Just Write

A Collection of Stories and Poems from
Just Write the Creative Writing Group of
Haywards Heath u3a

Just Write

Disclaimer
The characters and events portrayed in the stories and poems in this book are purely fictional. Any similarity to persons living or dead is unintentional. While the writers are members of u3a, any opinions or beliefs stated or implied in the work are personal to the individual author and should not be regarded as endorsed by the u3a

ISBN: 9798753739186

Introduction

Just Write is the Creative Writing Group of Haywards Heath u3a. I had the privilege of taking over leadership of this talented group of writers in March 2020 when Pat Stanhope, our leader for many years, decided to put down her pen for the time being.

The group meets monthly, when we read and review our writing based on a 'prompt' given at the previous meeting. It's quite amazing to see the diversity of writing which comes out of a single prompt – From moving and evocative poetry to amazing short stories which are emotional, amusing, exciting, sometimes challenging and always a pleasure to read. Some members are working on personal memoirs and we are happy to give them support and encouragement too.

We hope you will enjoy this anthology of our work. It covers a wide spectrum so I'm sure there will be something for everyone.

March 2020 saw the start of the first Covid lock-down; some of our members were not comfortable with remote communication and decided to take a break from writing. As a result, our numbers diminished, so to drum up some interest I issued a challenge to u3a members to tell a story in just ten words. The response was encouraging and we welcomed several new members to the group.

This collection includes a selection of ten-word poems and stories written by group members. It's astonishing that such a few words can tell so much of a story. I think they are quite special and have highlighted them throughout the book. I hope you will enjoy them as much as I do.

It's been an absolute pleasure editing this collection of our writings and I'm proud to have been able to put it together for you. Whether you read it all from cover to cover, or dip into it as the mood takes you, I'm sure you will be delighted.

By the way, in case you're not sure what u3a is all about, there's a brief explanation on page 150.

Enjoy!

Gordon Reece Davies

Just Write

Acknowledgements

Nigel Hall has kindly put in many hours of painstaking work proof-reading this book and then formatting for use on electronic devices, and advising/assisting in the publication process. We are truly grateful for all your help, Nigel.

Thanks also to Andrew Critchell L.R.P.S. for allowing the extract from his review of the Chailey Airshow to be included in Mary Richard's piece.

Dedication

Dedicated to our readers, albeit coerced loved ones, the ridiculously optimistic, hopelessly misguided or the true patron of literature; whichever you may be, welcome to this first edition.

Just Write

CONTENTS

Just Write

Just Write

Consciousness   *Richard Hughes*

Finding out who I was and if the same
As those who brought me here, soon was my job.
The struggle to assert myself became
Shouting Mummy with increasing sobs
Worked well at summoning the aid indeed
Why is? How are shoes? When do I be growd?
Rarely got me the information needed
Making me question my grasp of the code.

Food, shelter, nurturing, support, the State
Finds me in employment and with a wife.
Now, it's me who responds to cries and, later,
Whys and wherefores.
However, for all the work done before
I've no idea how I'm going to perform.

* * *

Richard Hughes

Since being praised for imaginative writing at Primary school, there has been a notion in my mind that one day I'll write something to get more praise. This may still happen. On and off, during my life, I've been in writing groups and enjoyed being encouraged and encouraging others to write for pleasure.

Working in a variety of engineering firms: an apprenticeship with a bottling plant manufacturer, the Science Museum, electrical training on a TOPS course, working for a medical equipment manufacturer (making neonatal ventilators) and another firm making filling machines has been my working life.

Having a lovely wife and four great children is my main preoccupation, but writing is still an interest.

A Curator   *Richard Hughes*

She's here, I can feel the heat of her, I could turn over
and watch her breathe.
Just wait. In case I'm dreaming again; best wait
Sunlight, an open-door silhouetting Mother
Standing there. No cover, Venus rising, holding open
hands to herself.
Oh, shit this is a dream, and I'm alone.

Five o'clock, up we get, start tea
Most important meal of the day; a cup of tea.
Cold though, but glad I had the wit not to get
undressed last night.
Still clever enough to look after myself.
No bloody home care visit for me.

To the bathroom, past piles of her clothes, stacks of
newspapers,
A museum of electrical appliances and tools of various
trades.
Enough stuff to cover almost all the floor.
Getting about requires local knowledge only one safe
place
For each foot fall; an avalanche waiting for the
hesitant or wary.

/Over

3

Delicate soft green, on the surface of the sink at a tide mark

In the static, stagnant water that remains.

The low light of evening makes it hard to really understand how urgent

And of what nature the work to be done in here is.

I'll be back, like Arnie, with purpose intent.

Backdoor might yield, now spring is here.

Clever Dad, ran a cable out to the garden with a switch on this wall.

Click.

A dim yellow at the shed window making thoughts

Of pumping bike tyres getting ready for an escape.

It smells different here and sticky underfoot.

In this Den, this cave, this retreat, home for the Hearth.

Ah! TV, flickering away nicely, sharing the world and other stuff.

A good and faithful servant when the electric meter has a belly full.

Sofaing, sprawling, board gaming, play that avoids disrespecting the figurines.

Hall mirror telling lies again, showing Father, or Uncle Bert.

Odd. Never me.

Plenty of hooks for coats and an umbrella stand that's empty, the coats

Stiff and dusty faded to unbelievable near transparency can't ever have had

Living things to animate or articulate them, just been props for museums.

4

Aftershave almost, but not quite, in Paul's room

Janet's has fragrance and lovely things on hangers,
some with polyethene, and

Books in jackets, ring binders, some stuffed soft toy
creatures.

When she comes, she will be mad if she thinks I've
been looking.

I have.

The day centre tomorrow, one day, one tomorrow day
in the afternoon.

Mum's grave another, when it's overcast and grey,
suitably dank a miserable day

The Doctor has not seen me, I've not seen him or she;
I do believe that Doctors kill

Off parents with their kindnesses and pills. They don't
mean to but they do

The Job Centre and Parliament, the Town Hall the
Hospital may or may not feel a duty of

Care for me

I know I have no feel for them.

* * *

Polly Paice

THIS IS ME

I've always been fascinated with words, probably because from a young age you would find me cross-legged on the floor reading a book.

I loved to write poems. My first achievement was to have my poem published in the school magazine. I never looked back from that. I remember my English teacher saying that I could paint a picture with my words. My teenage years were too busy for me to write much; then children took my time.

I re-discovered my love of words once the children became independent. I wrote a book of poems and meditations, but never did much with them. Joining the u3a writing group was a new challenge of writing short stories which I enjoy very much. I submitted a mixture of poems and short stories for this book. I hope you like them.

The Shadow   *Polly Paice*

She's dancing there before me, elusive, ethereal
I hold out my hand to her, but her I cannot feel.
So close, but so elusive, forever out of touch
I'm happy when she's near me, I like her very much

I turn, now she's behind me, she's playing with me, toying
She walks beside me for a while, then fades, it's so annoying
She loves the sun, and in the woods, she dances round me, flying
And I cannot catch up with her no matter how hard I'm trying

She hides in the flickering light, she's right there, then takes flight
She's gone now, merging with shadows of the approaching night
On the street, she's back again under shining lights
Behind, beside, in front of me, dancing with delight

I find comfort in her presence as I go about my day
I miss her when she's not there in dull wet winter days
She's me, my other self, the one who's free
To frolic in the sunlight, I do wish that were me.

Gordon Reece Davies

I used to write a lot of reports and memos, minutes of meetings and plenty of similar formal stuff when I was working. When I retired from managing the accounts department of a firm of heating engineers, five years ago, I resolved to start writing something a bit more entertaining.

I still haven't got round to writing that novel I promised myself, but maybe one day... meanwhile I'm enjoying my role as leader of the Writing Group and scribbling down one or two short stories.

I'm married with two lovely grown-up daughters and a delightful two-year old granddaughter. Besides my family, my passions are dinghy sailing, my classic car and of course, writing.

Digby's Shadow   *Gordon Reece Davies*

It was a sunny Monday in mid-April when Felix Digby first noticed something strange. It was one of those glorious April mornings, still and crisp with a hint of warmth in the sunshine. There were daffodils and tulips in the front gardens of Caradon Road and somewhere nearby a bird was singing.

Felix, who preferred to be known by his old RAF nickname of 'Digger' was on his way to the shops for his morning paper. Halfway there, and he began to feel uncomfortable. It was a strange, indefinable feeling of unease, as though he was being watched. He stopped and turned to see whether someone was following him. There was a man in a grey coat about a hundred yards behind him on the opposite side of the road. Digger thought he had seen him before, but he couldn't think where. There were sparrows nesting in the nearby hedge, Digger thought maybe it was their comings and goings that had spooked him; he walked on.

As he reached the corner of the road the feeling came back, if anything stronger. Again, he stopped and looked around. The man in the grey coat was no longer there but, as he turned, from the corner of his eye Digger sensed a movement. His head spun round and he realised it had been nothing more than his own shadow moving against the whitewashed wall of the shop.

Digger and his wife, Carrie, had bought the bungalow in Caradon Road nearly twenty years ago, when Digger had sold his building business and retired. It was almost three years since Carrie had passed away and Digger had surprised himself at his ability to keep things going. True, the bungalow was no longer as spotlessly clean as Carrie used to keep it, and he didn't eat quite as well, but the place was still meticulously tidy and he hadn't starved or poisoned himself.

He enjoyed his daily walk down to the little shop on the corner to collect his newspaper. Over the years, the shop had changed hands several times. The present owners, Mr. Shar and his wife were a friendly couple and Digger always looked forward to exchanging a few words with them.

"Good morning, Digger and how are you," Mr. Shar was already retrieving Digger's Daily Mail from amongst the small pile of reserved periodicals on the shelf behind the counter. He passed the newspaper across. "How did you go on at the hospital on Friday?"

"Not good I'm afraid. There was a shadow on the X-Ray; it's a tumour, they say it's cancer."

"I'm sorry to hear that, but they can do wonderful things with cancer these days."

"Not for me. Look, I'm going to be eighty-five next month. At my age they won't operate. Radiotherapy might give me an extra month or so, but I can't see the point of going through all that for just a few weeks more."

"I'm so sorry."

"No need to be, I've had a good long life. I did two tours in bombers during the war with the angel of death standing at my shoulder, so I have no fears on that score; whenever it comes, I'll be ready."

"I don't know if I would be as brave – you're a strong man Digger – will there be anything else?"

"Just these please." Digger picked up a packet of Polo mints and paid Mr. Shar.

Over the course of the next month, Digger continued to have the feeling that he was being followed. As a rear-gunner on heavy bombers he had developed a very acute peripheral vision which had become almost a sixth sense. He couldn't be sure whether the discomfort could be explained away by small movements all around him or the side-effects of the pain-killing drugs he was taking; or whether he was actually being followed. He would turn around and the man in the grey coat would be in sight. Sometimes nearer, sometimes further away. He still couldn't remember where he had seen him before. It seemed as though the uncomfortable feeling was worse when Digger turned around and the man was nowhere to be seen.

* * *

"Do you think he's a stalker?" asked Mr. Shar

"Oh no I don't think so, he's not threatening-like, he's more of a shadow – that's what I call him – my shadow."

"Have you told your son about this?"

"My son's away in New York, on business, but he'd only say I'm going barmy and the doctor says it could be hallucinations due to the drugs, but I know what I've seen. I just wish I knew where I've seen him before."

"Have you tried speaking to him?" asked Mr. Shar.

"I've called across the road but he doesn't seem to hear me."

Mrs. Shar had been listening to the conversation.

"It must be so uncomfortable for you, Digger, you know we can deliver your paper for you if it's starting to get too much for you; there wouldn't be a charge." She looked across at her husband.

"No, ... No charge for you Digger."

"That's very kind of you both, but as long as I've got the strength, I enjoy my little morning walk." Digger pocketed his change and turned towards the door.

"Well, you just take care Digger, I'll see you tomorrow."

Digger went next door, to the little supermarket and bought some beef mince and potatoes to make himself a cottage pie for dinner and a packet of digestives to go with his mid-morning cuppa. He stepped out of the shop and looked across the road; the man in the grey coat was there again.

"Hey, just a minute...." Digger waved his arm and called. He set off across the road to speak to the man.

* * *

The driver of the Transit van had no chance to stop in time. The impact threw Digger back towards the shop and his head hit the edge of the pavement.

The paramedics did their best to stabilise Digger before taking him to hospital. Digger slipped in and out of consciousness and was vaguely aware that the man in the grey coat had accompanied him in the ambulance and was waiting outside the Critical-Care Room while the doctor treated him. Eventually the doctor moved away.

The man in the grey coat stepped up to the bedside and gently placed his hand on Digger's arm. Digger opened his eyes.

"Who are you?" he asked.

"You know who I am Digger; I was right beside you on all those missions, sometimes you called me your guardian angel and sometimes you called me the Shadow, the Greeks and the Romans called me the ferryman. You couldn't see me, but I was always there for you... and your comrades. I was right beside you when Carrie passed and I was there for her too. Just as I'm here for you now. When you're ready, we'll make the journey together."

Digger closed his eyes.

"I'm ready now."

* * *

Superfine Snake Oil
(a bridge to the Middle Ages)

Richard Hughes

All of St. Donald has been saved.

His Mother, Doctor and himself did this wonderful work.

Carefully maintaining, against the days of need, his essence.

And, since the passing, these days are now.

His bones ethically ground,

Flesh carefully dried,

Excretions all 12,000 kg desiccated,

Hair: head and quiff, lashes, brow, arms and legs, back, groin, feet,

Nails clipped since his holy birth.

Mucus (as above)

All organs

Milled and coalesced into a paste.

A relic of First order as it is himself, not a supplicant or substitute

You must buy a $10 tube of Donessence

To smooth onto a sore, an open wound, an orifice.

Also, troublesome items involving spiritual, political and fiscal matters can be treated.

For $100, 500mg tubs can be had, to spread over whole persons.

In remembrance of Him this will be done.

Mike Gardiner

Having had an interesting working life, divided between
assessing public liability risks in a large insurance group
and teaching theology in western Brazil, I am now
enjoying a retirement which includes leading the u3a
Opera Group, playing bridge, walking the Downs with my
lovely wife Jean and being part of the exciting church
family at All Saints Lindfield. And of course, seeking to
improve my ability to write creatively, when I get time!

Reflections of an Aged Terrorist
Mike Gardiner

Joel the prophet said that our old men would dream dreams... I guess they always have... There seems nothing else left for me to do; half-blind, with a wheezy chest... You will forgive a man who's coming up to his threescore years and ten, won't you?

I've seen dreams bring fire to the belly of young men, and I've seen those dreams shattered, hopes ground in the dust. Why? Because we wanted to be free. Yes, freedom! Is that a crime?

What did Moses say to Pharaoh? Yes, that's right – "Set my people free!" and we worship him as a national hero. But when young men, some still in their teens, took up arms against a modern-day Pharaoh, our useless religious leaders sneered and called them 'dagger-men.' Worse still, they betrayed us to our enemies, conniving with them against us, calling us revolutionaries deserving of being strung upon a cross. Yes, I know all about it.

You've recognised me, haven't you? Yes, Barabbas the great escaper, that's me. Forty years ago, my moment of fame. Reprieved at the last minute. I tell you; I couldn't believe it! Walking free while that harmless pacifist from Nazareth got nailed up in my place. Couldn't understand it. Still don't know to this day why the religious toffs were so happy to see me go free. But I'll tell you who weren't happy – the Roman soldiers.

D'you know what I enjoyed most on that day? It was seeing the faces of those men! They... were... absolutely... livid! I grinned at them as I walked to freedom, those heathen louts who'd finally trapped me after I'd led them a hell of a dance for more than a year.

My name was known throughout the 12th Legion – top of their Wanted list. Might have had something to do with the fact that I'd knifed one or two of them along the way, of course. Wish I'd got a lot more. Why not? They were enemies of Yahweh, oppressors of God's chosen people. Gideon didn't hesitate to slaughter the Midianite invaders. Samson made sure he took a lot of Philistines with him, didn't he? Judas Maccabeus slaughtered those Greeks who were bent on destroying our ancient religion.

You may have heard people say I lost my nerve after my amazing escape from death. Truth is, they were watching my every move. Two of them cornered me in an alley once – left me half dead. They made sure I wasn't going to give them any more trouble! I lay low after that, and a rumour went around that I'd joined those followers of the Galilean...

They think he's still alive y'know, come back from the dead or something. He talked about freedom too, I did go and hear him once. We all talked about freedom in those days, mind you. Just that we all had different ideas.

The bigwigs in Jerusalem said we had to go with the flow, collaborate with the Romans, you scratch my back, I'll scratch yours. If it wasn't for you women present, I'd tell you what I thought of that. They knew which side their bread was buttered on; getting fat while the rest of us were taxed up to our eyeballs, paying not only for the Temple but helping to keep Caesar's wine cellars well stocked... They called that freedom!

The Pharisees said that if we all obeyed the Laws of Moses all the time, God would come down and throw out all the heathen. Fat chance of that – the Pharisees were as bad as the rest of us, if you ask me. That dreamer from Nazareth, he seemed to be saying that if we wanted to be free, we should all be his followers and start praying for our enemies. Huh! Catch me praying for those soldiers? Talk about unrealistic!

Y'know, we invited him to join us – we'd have made a great team ... he had the country folk eating out of his hand! We got one of our men into his inner circle, did you know that? Sad, poor old Judas. Topped himself because he saw that the Galilean had missed his chance to take Jerusalem by storm.

And here I am ... older and wiser. Yes, and much sadder. I stayed clear of this latest uprising, got out of the city sharpish when I saw what was coming. And now ... oh, you foreigners wouldn't understand what that holy city means to us. Why even the Galilean wept – they say he could see what was coming, though we didn't believe him. But he's been proved right. Our beautiful city devastated and thousands slaughtered. All because we wanted freedom!

* * *

Because that's what Barabbas was; one of those who believed in violent rebellion against the Roman oppressors. He is mentioned in all four Gospels (see Mark 15:1-15 for example), and no serious scholar denies his historicity, though no-one knows what happened to him afterwards. The Jewish uprising finally happened in AD66 and was brutally put down by the Roman army, with the city of Jerusalem destroyed and hundreds of thousands of Jewish deaths. My imagined soliloquy takes place shortly after the carnage finished in AD70.

The Choirmaster's Bicycle
Polly Paice

Look, there's the choirmaster's bicycle.
Parked behind the shed
Of number seven Gallop Mews,
It really must be said.

It seems to be there often,
When her husband is away.
Or leaned against the garden fence
It's almost every day.

I bumped into the choirmaster's bicycle
It really gave me a fright
It's outside Mrs. S today
It was Mrs. B's last night.

That cycle really gets around
It has a mind of its own
It was next to Mrs. B's bicycle
At least it's not alone.

It's behind number seven's shed again
What is it doing there?
Perhaps he and Mrs. Gallagher
Are having an affair.

As I followed him to Mrs. B's
I noticed on the gate
A poster proclaiming the ladies' choir
Were singing at the local fete.

I was ashamed of myself for thinking
The choirmaster was doing wrong
Especially as I walked past the church
And heard the choir in song.

The day of the fete was sunny
And the choir's song hung in the air
As the choirmaster bowed with his pupils
I knew I had been very unfair.

In the weeks after the performance
The bike was not to be seen
Not outside Mrs. B or outside Mrs. S
Or by the hedge at seventeen.

When I next see the choirmaster
I'll confess my wicked thoughts
And I hope I'll still go to heaven
When my suspicions all came to naught.

Still thinking of my unfairness
The church clock struck eleven
But wait, there's the choirmasters bicycle
Behind the shed, again, at number seven.

* * *

10 Word Poem

Contact
By Richard Hughes

Forty years

Finding lenses you drop

For me,

Your slave

Autumn

Hazel Lintott

Earthy scents and swaying breezes lift my senses up above

The laden hedges, golden treetops, to the red and soft'ning skies.

This is when my heart beats faster, sweet excitement fills my veins.

Now is time for new beginnings; new life primed as old life dies.

See the seeds in fallen apples or the spores from fungi damp

Dropping down among the leaf-mould where they start a journey new.

Children love to take the treasured, shiny nuts and leaves so red,

But I would leave them, flowers of springtime, fruits of harvest next year due.

In the midst of life decaying lay the promises of health

And stronger life, from old lives given, a blueprint set from ages past.

Let the icy winds and hailstorms beat their rhythms on the earth,

For underground new life is waiting; autumn's seed awaits its birth.

Hazel Lintott

As a child and as a teenager I was fascinated with maps and loved hearing the stories behind places and how they came to be. This led to my work in the University of Sussex Cartographic Unit and to my study as a mature student for a Masters in Human Geography. I now particularly enjoy the poetry of John Clare (known in his time as the 'peasant poet') who painted detailed word pictures of his local area in Northamptonshire. Retirement and membership of the fantastic u3a has now encouraged me to try my hand at writing my own poetry, which often has a landscape theme.

Highlander

Hazel Lintott

She looks agitated. It is nearly 80 degrees and the dusty London pavement is like a hot griddle, baking everything that touches it. She drags herself slowly towards Euston Station. Her cases and backpack have been packed full; she is expecting to be away for a long time. She briefly wipes her forehead with the back of her hand. She is not comfortable in the stifling heat of the city in the summer.

As she waits with the small crowd at the lights to cross the road you can catch a glimpse of her tense face beneath a head of thick and softly curling auburn hair. Her skin, normally pale and almost translucent is flushed to an uncomfortable pink.

After her arrival in the city a little under a decade ago she had been moderately successful at work, but she had never really settled happily into life in London. She was disturbed by a growing assurance that she had to leave. Something was pulling her back. As the voice became more persistent, she felt more and more ill at ease. So she had come to a decision.

She boards an inter-city train and finds her booked seat. After settling her luggage into the rack at the end of the carriage she settles back into her seat and lets the swaying of the train slowly relax her tight limbs.

The cool air-conditioning makes her feel more comfortable as she watches the last remnants of London flash by and fade into the distance. For a brief moment a smile flickers across her face. She is on her way.

The landscape changes as the hours tick by, familiar sounding towns are reached, doors slam and people shuffle past with their bags and children trailing behind. Soon the train is speeding northwards again, tilting at the curves, rushing through tunnels and cuttings and sweeping across broad estuaries with sandy shorelines and heather-clad hillsides. She leans towards the window to savour the changing panorama unfolding before her, then checks the time. Not long.

* * *

The last bus that afternoon drops her off on a deserted road where the bare moorlands stretch up into the mist. The sudden silence hits her and she takes a moment to orientate herself. It's raining with a gentle persistence – just like it had been when she was last here, exactly 10 years ago. The cool air has the same earthy freshness she remembers so well.

She gathers her bags and turns to walk up a rutted track, avoiding the rivulets coursing their way down. Her hair is clinging together in dark, wet strands but she doesn't notice. Her face becomes flushed again, but this time with the soft dampness that is enveloping her head. She walks up into the mist where her whole world is just a small circle, and nothing else seems to exist.

Where the track begins to slope downwards again she stops and takes a small package from her backpack. She leaves her bags at the side of the track and starts running down the hillside. She can smell the water in the loch ahead, a smell she had once known and loved – but which she now feared.

Suddenly there was the water, calm as ever, deceptively calm. She holds the package up to her face as her tears mix with the rain and dampen it. She throws it far out into the water and stands and watches as the ripples spread wider and wider until they melt back into the calm green surface.

She stands for a long time looking out across the loch, then slowly turns and walks back, picks up her bags and makes towards a small stone building above her.

The bothy is used by hikers for overnight stays, just as she and Abby had done all those years ago. She sits at a table, opens her bag and takes out a photo of a smiling auburn-haired girl aged about 9 years. She looks out the window, down towards the loch, and feels a tremble in her heart. Tomorrow she will get the bus into town and begin a new life. A welcome peace overcomes her. This is where she belongs.

* * *

Just Deserts

The prompt for this piece was to write a ballad. I don't normally write poetry, so it was quite a challenge especially as it requires a strict meter and rhyming scheme.

I started with the idea of the 'other woman' at her lover's funeral but feeling excluded by the family who barely cared about him anyway. As I played around with the idea and started to work out a few rhymes I realised it might work as a comic piece and it began to take on a life of its own. It's just a bit of fun really, but it works for me and I hope you enjoy it!

Gordon Davies

Just Deserts   *Gordon Reece Davies*

St Mark's was full, they all turned up
    But very few would cry,
To say farewell to reckless Jack
    Good riddance and goodbye.

The eulogy was given by
    Professor Wills, Jack's boss
"I just can't say how much I am
    So sorry for his loss."

"He was the nicest man I knew,
    A really clever boffin,
Whose pioneering work on poison gas
    Has ended in this coffin."

"We all thought well of him 'tis true,"
    His widow dabbed her eyes
To hear his colleague, stand up there
    And utter all those lies.

He hadn't liked Jack, but perhaps
    He thought it would be cruel
To tell her to her face this day
    They'd all called him a fool.

/Over

27

He'd paid no heed to safety rules,
    He'd done it his own way
And Frank Sinatra's famous song
    Would play for him this day.

"The final hymn," the vicar said,
    "Is called Abide with me."
'Let's get it over with,' he thought,
    'It's nearly time for tea.'

While coffin to the graveyard went
    To Frankie's dulcet tones,
The mourners bowed their heads, some wept,
    But others checked their phones.

They all filed past the final pew
    Where thin and rather pale,
A woman dressed in black was sat
    In tears behind a veil.

She heard the vicar's final verse,
    She watched the coffin drop
Into the grave and then they all
    Put earth and flowers on top.

With due decorum, back they went
    Then jumped in cars with haste
To miss the pub and all that food
    Would be a dreadful waste.

In tears, she stumbled to the grave
    The Other Woman, all in black.
She said a prayer, she shed more tears
    And said "I miss you, Jack."

And by and by, Another Other came
    But she was dressed in blue.
She looked her rival up and down
    And said "I loved him too."

She whispered in the other's ear
    "I know how much it hurts,
But when all's said and done, my friend,
    He got his just deserts."

* * *

Norma Hall

I grew up in Zimbabwe but have lived in the UK since 2002. There are so many stories in life to tell and I feel my short stories reflect my background in the places I have lived, as well as my experience in social work – family therapy and children's mental health – in particular.

Married with 2 daughters and a grandchild, I have enjoyed many u3a activities since my retirement, as well as travelling, which I love.

I published my own short story book in early 2021 – My Country and Other Stories.

Happy Valentine's   *Norma Hall*

As Marta ran out of the shaded alleyway, she was almost blinded by the bright sun and the carefree beach scene that confronted her. Raising her hand to shade her eyes, she stared at the brightly coloured umbrellas, the thick towels and the tanned bodies lying spread out on them; bikinis and big boobs on the women, short trunks and amazing torsos on the guys. A few were fatter cigar-smoking older men, their wives splayed out on sunbeds, still glued to their mobile phones despite the startlingly beautiful sea and sand that surrounded them.

Recollecting her dilemma, Marta shook off her initial feeling of the unreality of the scene before her and looking left, then right and seeing no one in pursuit, she turned towards the harbour and the bustle of numerous market traders operating between the smaller and larger boats moored there, near to the Museum of the Revolution.

She needed to think and think fast! But how had it all started and where was it going to end? This was meant to be her long-awaited Cuban holiday and now it was turning into more of a nightmare instead!

Crouching behind the harbour wall, her knees clasped tight in front of her, Marta closed her eyes and thought back. It seemed like only yesterday she had been happily packing and looking forward to her Valentine's holiday. It was a day she normally dreaded as when everyone else got cards or flowers, she pretty much never received a thing.

It wasn't that she wasn't attractive with her fair hair and classic face, but Marta was quite shy and since she'd moved to the city, her job as a PA for a rather old fashioned two-man company, meant she didn't really get much of a chance to meet anyone.

For years now, on 14th February she'd dreaded that anxious questioning from her mother's weekly telephone call as to how the day had been for her. Her mother had long given up asking her 'the actual' question as the answer was always the same, but still there was that hint of disappointment that once again, there was nothing to tell.

But this year was going to be different, Marta was sure. She'd met Sebastian online and they'd met up a few times. He seemed quite nice and at least he was interested in her, a little older than Marta but good looking in a dark haired, brooding sort of way, although there didn't seem that much that they had in common. He was easy to talk to though, charming really and they'd shared a few laughs and he'd clearly enjoyed taking her to dinner, showing off his superior culinary knowledge and to others, her fair-haired attractiveness.

It was he who had suggested the trip. He was visiting old friends in Havana, and she could stay in a city hotel fairly inexpensively. It was a beautiful place; they could meet up and he'd show her around. The night before, she'd arrived and so far, her stay at the Casa Pedro-Maria had exceeded her expectation. The hotel staff were friendly and warm, the food spicy and unusual and she'd enjoyed a good, few glasses of wine before retiring early, tired after her long flight.

The next morning, Marta got ready with a feeling of excitement she hadn't felt for a long time. She knew they might meet up later with Sebastien's friends and remembered to pack the present she'd brought for them in her handbag. English tea in a pretty tin, which Sebastian had recommended and bought for her to give them. He'd suggested they meet at the National Capitol Building, (El Capitolio), an iconic public building in the Paseo Prado and it was there she was headed, clutching her first Valentine's Day card, which had been waiting for her at the old wooden reception desk when she handed in her room keys after breakfast.

The taxi the hotel had called for her was a colourful 1950's model, painted a gaudy purple with its taxi sign in the window, which like most taxis in Havana were usually shared and could pick up others along the same route – 'collectivos' they were known as.

The old Spanish architecture and vibrant colours of the buildings they passed, made the whole journey have something of a dream-like quality as she turned her eyes away from the window and opened up the card. It was a rather old-fashioned card, frilly with a large red heart with several arrows through it. Inside, it was unsigned but a message, looking a bit like it had been cut out of old newspaper print, read unmistakably, 'Dying for your love.'

Marta looked at the words in amazement, perplexed as to the implications. It must be from Sebastian of course, but rather over the top, wasn't it? It didn't really sound like him and neither was she sure she wanted things to move that fast anyway!

Her thoughts distracted, Marta hadn't taken much notice when the taxi pulled over to let two other hard-looking, young men get into the taxi next to her.

"Nice card," one of them said, roughly, in English, peering over at it.

"Yes, and we know who will be dying if you don't hand over that package soon enough," the other threatened, one hand on her arm and the other prodding Marta in her side.

Marta gasped. Thinking back over it all now, it seemed so obvious! Her astonishment had helped her at the time however, as she looked unknowingly at the men and fearing they were there to rob her, shouted and rapped on the taxi driver's window.

Then leaping from the car as it screeched to a stop and making a bee line for the darkened alleyways before her. She had taken a quick glimpse over her shoulder and seen the men also exit the taxi and come running after her.

When her breathing slowed and her fear was a little more controlled, the tears came as she thought of the deceit she must have suffered and the Valentine's Day card she'd finally received, being fake. How could Sebastian have used her like that?

Making sure she wasn't being watched, she carefully took out the present from her handbag and threw it violently into the sea; relieved to see what she now thought must be some sort of dangerous and illegal drug, floating away. Coming out from its wrapping, the pretty tin of tea was taken off, bobbing on a small receding wave into the Harbour.

At the reception desk of the Casa Pedro-Maria, the clerk at reception, was scratching his head looking worried, as the now angry men who'd asked him to give the card to the 'English senorita who arrived last night,' had returned to discover it had been given to the wrong lady. Marta would have been relieved to know there was no one coming after her now.

Meanwhile Sebastian, waiting outside El Capitolio, was glancing at his watch and wondering why Marta was so late. He'd told his friends all about her and was sure they'd like her and the nice English tea she'd brought for them. He was getting worried now as he stood with a lovely bunch of red roses and a card in his hands for what he hoped would be the first of many of his Valentine's days offerings for Marta.

The Concert Pianist   *Polly Paice*

The stage was bare... except for a magnificent grand piano, centre stage. Caught in the rays of the sun from the ornate stained-glass windows, bathed in rainbows, no curtain, no spotlight, no orchestra in the pit, just an empty stage, the piano and the rainbows.

The auditorium was empty, quiet and dark, but there were ghosts... Oh yes, there were ghosts! As Helen stood on the empty stage, she could hear the rustle of people, and the gentle murmur of conversation. She could smell the slight mustiness of the seats, mingled with perfume from the elegant ladies in the audience. She could feel the electric anticipation in the air. She felt alive again; just for that one moment, she felt alive.

The piano seemed to taunt her from its multicoloured cloud, 'Come play me,' it seemed to whisper. With an angry shout, she fled from the stage, tears streaming from her eyes.

* * *

Helen had been a child prodigy, playing the piano at a ridiculously early age. From the age of nine, she even composed her own music. Music school was a doddle for her; she passed every exam with flying colours. By the time she was 18 she was a renowned concert pianist and composer. Feted by the famous, she even played before the kings and queens of Europe.

She met the love of her life, Emanuel, a tenor of renown when she was twenty, they were engaged to be married the next spring. Her life was perfect, until that fateful day.

There were rainbows that day, shining bright over the mountains, the brightest colours she had ever seen.

"That is our rainbow," said Emanuel, "Whenever we see rainbows, we will be blessed, that's what my mother always says."

"Our blessed rainbow," she snuggled up to Emanuel. Just as she said it, clouds over the mountaintop obscured the rainbow, leaving only a grey mist. She shivered,

"This is an omen," she said.

"You are too fanciful" said Emanuel in his deep accented voice, "We are blessed; in two weeks we will be married, what is more blessed than that?" But still she shivered; a deep sense of foreboding came over her, which she could not shift.

Soon, the clouds parted again. The sun came out, but there was no rainbow. They continued walking down the mountain, picking their way carefully down the rocky path. The scent of wild flowers was in the air, and the fresh mountain air filled their lungs, invigorating them as they walked. It was cooler up in the mountains, but the sun now shone steadily, warming them as they descended.

It took a while to get to the valley, but once there, they had a leisurely lunch of the local delicacies. They sat in the sunshine, surrounded by magnificent mountains, and sampled the local liquors. It was a perfect day, but yet Helen could not shake-off the feeling of foreboding.

"We had better start back over the mountains before the cloud comes down," she said.

"It is a beautiful day, the cloud will not come down before nightfall," said Emanuel, "let's stay a while longer." They strolled around the village, looking in local tourist shops, which sold lace and wicker work.

"I would like that," said Helen "But we couldn't carry it on the motorbike."

"Yes, we can," said Emanuel; "we can tie it on to the pannier." Purchase duly made, they made their way to where they had parked their motorbike, and proceeded to tie the wicker chair on to the back of the bike.

"It looks too big to carry on the bike" said Helen but

Emanuel was adamant it would be OK. They set off down the steep windy roads, Emanuel was more careful than usual because of the large load on the back. Every now and then they met vehicles coming the other way and pulled over to let them by. The drop was steep on one side, and Helen was a little frightened, but Emanuel, being a macho man, just laughed at her.

"We'll be fine," he said. They finally reached level ground, much to Helen's relief, and she began to relax when suddenly a coach came round the bend. It narrowly missed the bike, but it hit the chair on the back, and then there was blackness...

* * *

Helen woke to a light in her eyes, and a kind face.
"You are back with us," said a heavily accented voice.
"Where am I?"
"You are in Santa Jose Hospital," said the doctor.
"Emanuel?" she cried "How is he?" The doctor hesitated,
"I will find out for you, but now you must rest. You have serious injuries."
"I want to speak to Emanuel," Helen was beginning to get agitated.
"You must not upset yourself," said the doctor, "we will speak later when you are feeling a little better. I will give you something to help you relax."
"But I don't want..." but it was too late, the doctor had given her an injection; she was beginning to get sleepy.

* * *

Helen slept, but her sleep was disturbed by dreams; she was trying to get to Emanuel, but he was far away, she couldn't reach him no matter how hard she tried. He called to her, but he was fading, then he was gone. Helen was crying when she woke, the dream was too real. The nurse came to change her dressings and take her observations.

"Emanuel," said Helen "How is he?" The nurse's face looked sad,
"I will get the doctor to talk to you."

The doctor came. Emanuel's injuries had been too severe, and he had died earlier that morning.

"No!", Helen screamed, "No!" She felt her life was over, "I can't go on without Emanuel; it was my fault; I wanted that chair, I killed him."

Helen's injuries gradually healed: her physical injuries anyway, but her mental state was fragile. She withdrew into herself, staying indoors, neglecting herself, not eating, and pining, pining for her love Emanuel. Her agent tried to get her to honour the engagements for her concerts, but Helen had vowed never to play the piano again.

* * *

She didn't know what had drawn her back to this theatre; it had been a voice in her head, telling her to play again. It had been so insistent that she had followed the voice to the theatre, and there she was. On that stage, with the rainbows.

"Our rainbows," came the voice, "play for me." With a surge of emotion, she knew it was Emanuel, somehow telling her it was time to start playing again.

Helen walked over to the piano, and opened the lid,

'I can't do this' she thought.

"Yes, you can," said the voice in her head.

She sat down on the stool, took a deep breath, and started to play. Gently at first, and hesitantly; but as she grew more confidant, the music became stronger. The melody spilled from her fingers, filling the auditorium with music so spiritual and melodious, it seemed to hang in the air and glitter like crystal droplets. Tears spilled from her eyes; she was alive again. She had come home.

* * *

10 Words

Lockdown Wedding
By Gordon Reece Davies

Grandma's dress and tiara.

Fairytale wedding fit for a princess.

This was inspired by the Lockdown wedding of Princess Beatrice.

Just Write

Carol Merrett

I'm married with two adult children, who have fled the nest, thus liberating my creative instincts!

Having written stories as a child, I am now finding my imagination lends itself to more poetic musings and reflections on the world around us. Walking in the beautiful Sussex countryside in every changing season – and in all weathers – has unleashed many emotions encouraging me to put pen to paper.

Lifeless
Carol Merrett

Shimmering, silky folds of loveliness floated before
me

As beautiful as an iridescent peacock
Shining in the sunlit room.

Salty tears streamed softly down my dew-blushed
cheeks

Memories invading my very soul.

Vibrant colours of green and silver, it hung there
limply,

Now emptied of its dazzling sparkle, its glossy beauty;

I could hear the rippling laughter that filled every fold,

Its spirit, its joy echoing loudly in the dusty, stillness
of my room.

I closed my eyes, inhaled the dusky perfume, still
lingering evocatively.

I flew back in time, listening, listening...

Remembering Maggie, Betty, Nancy and me...

A hot summer's evening filled with the headiness and
insouciance of youth.

The band struck up, strumming guitars, beating
drums, singing stridently;

Our feet tapping, our bodies swaying to the music;

Irresistibly drawn to the dance floor, we moved to its
pulsating beat

Caught up in the joy of our youth, carefree, our lives
stretching before us;

Maggie, Betty, Nancy and me.   */Over*

Flicking our skirts, twirling, swaying, giggling, the night stretched elastically before us;

Our dresses reflecting the bursting colours of the rainbow.

They crossed the floor, immaculately dressed, shiny shoes, twirly moustaches;

Bowed extravagantly to Maggie, Betty, Nancy... He turned to me.

Grabbed my hand, kissed it, his blue eyes gazing deeply into my soul;

"Mademoiselle, tu es si belle...quelle robe magnifique!"

Irresistibly, I smiled... the beginning and the end!

We danced, danced and danced again,

Words were unnecessary... I was bewitched and under His spell;

He was bewitched by my haunting green eyes;

Magnetically and magically drawn to each other,

Laughing, dancing, driving, dining;

All our lives entwined irrevocably from that memorable summer's night,

Maggie, Betty, Nancy and me.

Now, in silence, I stared at that dress again;

Our story seeping out from every seam;

Wandering from Paignton to Paris, Nice to Naples,

From balls to casinos, the ballet to opera, jazz to cabaret.

Music and laughter filling our every moment.

Dining on bubbles of champagne, caviar, foie gras, oysters;

Maggie, Betty, Nancy and me

Young people swept up in a world of dancing, dreams, extravagance, freedom.

Freedom?

Maggie, Betty, Nancy... but not for me!

Chained to that magnificent green dress... did I exist without it?

I blinked... remembering, haunted by his face;

His controlling magnetism

Always insisting, persisting... me resisting, existing;

Maggie, Betty, Nancy and me.

Until one moonlit night a powerful flash of anger filled me

Stubbornly, independently, irritably

I crumpled that shimmering green dress

Donning a wonderful, grey, faded, woollen garment.

He walked into the restaurant and I watched, I watched my prey

As His face filled with anger, contorting every contour, every line, every crease

/Over

Twitching spasms of rage rendering him speechless.

How we laughed!

Maggie, Betty, Nancy and me

Angrily slamming the door, He crashed out of our lives;

The spell had been broken, the magic woven by the silken threads torn.

An enchanted world changed for ever.

Touching the green silkiness again, I sighed, wiping the tears away.

Closing the doors of time, I whispered "adieu, au revoir."

* * *

This was inspired by my daughter's dress hanging in her room after a recent wedding. Looking at it after she had returned to York, it evoked many wonderful memories... but this piece is completely fictitious!

A Second Chance   *Norma Hall*

'To the blue eyed, gentle-looking man on the Jubilee line at Willesden Green, two years back on a sunny afternoon, when the train became loaded with a loud group of kids. We glanced around, then at each other and you smiled. That second was fun, hey?'

It was when she was alone looking down at her bruised arms, that Aisha* sometimes thought back to that day. The day she'd first seen Rudo*. It had been hot and noisy on the Jubilee line that afternoon, not the time or place you'd expect to feel your pulse quicken with a feeling of pending excitement at the glance from a stranger. He'd sat tall, good looking with his dark hair and eyes almost glowering, but then with a somewhat arrogant smirk and nod of his head, implied the question

"Are you up for it?"

He'd waited for her by the exit door, seeing if she would follow – expecting it, really. Aisha could barely believe it when she'd got up haltingly and then more decisively did exactly that. He'd taken her hand and led her up the escalator and out of the station, before finally turning towards her and giving a half smile and laugh.

'What was it about him? What was it about her, that had led to her doing that?' Aisha asked herself for the millionth time.

After they had been living together some months later on, Aisha began having vivid nightmares that terrified her, leaving her waking up sobbing and in need of actual physical comfort. Rudo had started up awake and asked her roughly what was wrong. He'd put his arms around her and she felt better but the dreams returned the night after that too, so she could hardly bear to try to get to sleep and felt more and more desperate. This just made Rudo angry, and she was reluctant to tell him of the fear she had that someone was in the flat or watching from outside, or of the stabbings and murders she was the victim of, if she did inadvertently fall asleep.

That first time they'd met, Rudo led Aisha to a nearby hotel in Kilburn where they drank in the bar before he led her upstairs. She's learnt he was Russian and working in the UK on business, but really it was his looks and confident sexuality that had captured her. She'd felt her body respond and switching off her mind, felt she had no other choice. The sex was rough, but all consuming. Aisha had never experienced anything like it and her whole self was encapsulated. Enraptured. In those sweaty, writhing, exuberant then orgasmic half hours, the two of them really did seem one.

He wanted her to stay but after a few days, conscience dictated that she at least try to return to her job. She did her best to resume where she'd suddenly left off but was continually tired by her lack of sleep and it was difficult to meet the demands of her pupils and her duties, as well as those of Rudo, who insisted they meet up every night. "But I have to work to pay the rent," Aisha explained. That was a mistake, and she was soon ensconced in Rudo's own flat and left alone for long hours each day, when he went about his own business.

With some freedom when Rudo was out, Aisha rang home but was met with too many questions and concern from her Turkish mother, who confirmed what she already knew about her father's reaction.

"You know how impulsive you can be Aisha! If you don't want an even worse situation, you'd better not call us anymore – at least for the present," her mother informed her. The second mistake was telling Rudo about this, and also of her planned visit to her friend Rosa. That was the first time his anger spilled over and he'd held her wrist, twisting it until she screamed and then banged her head hard against the wall.

"Can't you see what they're doing to you?!" he'd shouted. "We were happy before you tried to bring in others who can't understand our love." He'd pushed her away and gone out. Tired and upset, Aisha cried and in her muddled thoughts, wondered if she really was to blame. There was no one to turn to though and her question was unanswered.

At times, things were better. When Rudo was in a better mood, they went out together more. He didn't question her when she went out shopping and the feelings she'd felt for him returned. She never met any of his work colleagues or friends though and Rudo was always tight lipped when she raised the subject. If she overstepped the mark or tried to do more than she was 'allowed,' it was instantly different and depending on the circumstances, his anger would spill over into verbal abuse followed by hitting, punching, head banging or even kicking one time. And all the while, Rudo would blame her for making him have to take such actions.

The instances began to get worse and more frequent over the ensuing months. Aisha now wondered where it would all end. Her nightmares had returned and she knew instinctively she was in real danger.

'Where had it all started,' she asked herself again? Aisha's thoughts strayed back to that day on the train. She'd been dissatisfied with her life, her Turkish parents were strict and she didn't go out after returning each day from her teaching job at a school in West Hampstead. Her sister was already married to a much older man, a business partner of her father's and had three children. Aisha, worried that she would be next, was eager to do anything to get out of it. Life was passing her by and the only excitement she was experiencing was through the romances she read about in magazines, saw on TV or through her mobile phone.

She had enjoyed her job though and although the students could be loud and even rude at times, they were at least alive and could be fun. Some of the staff there were alright too. One of them, Peter, had been especially nice to her. He was amusing and the kids liked him.

She thought back to the fateful day she'd met Rudo, when she and Peter had been escorting some of their art students to the Tate Modern. Peter had such nice blue eyes and he'd smiled at her above the din the kids were making. Rosa would have said she was just being silly and romantic once again, but she couldn't help thinking how much better it would have been if she could go back in time and have a second chance. Wistfully, she doodled idly on some paper:

'To the blue eyed, gentle- looking man on the Jubilee line at Willesden Green, two years back on a sunny afternoon, when the train became loaded with a loud group of kids. We glanced around, then at each other and you smiled. That second was fun, hey?'

The door opened suddenly and Rudo stalked in...

* *Aisha – Arabic/Muslim/Hindu name meaning 'life, living, vivacious, prosperous'*
  Rudo – Short for Rudolph, of Germanic origin meaning 'glory-wolf

* * *

A Damp Squib   *Mike Gardiner*

"Not the kind of bread to use when preparing a snack –
nine letters." Martin looked up wearily from War and
Peace, where he was trying to sort out who was related
to whom among the myriad characters in Tolstoy's
saga. Why on earth did Russians all have three names?
And why had his daughter, Susan, given her mother a
book of cryptic crosswords for her birthday when Betty
liked nothing more complicated than a Maeve Binchy
book to curl up in an armchair with? Dragging his mind
back from 19th century St Petersburg, he asked Betty
to repeat the clue. He thought for a moment.

"It's quite an easy one really, dear. What's the
opposite of a snack?"

"A big meal?" she said tentatively.

"Nearly there … remember … type of bread?"

"Whole … meal," she cried, in the sort of voice that
Archimedes must have used for shouting Eureka!
"Merci beaucoup, dear," trilled Betty.

Martin tried to immerse himself once more in the
build-up to the battle of Austerlitz, but he couldn't
concentrate on the complicated lives of Tolstoy's
characters and found his mind wandering back to the
events of that day and what might have been.

It wasn't that he no longer loved Betty. She still had
that gentle voice he'd fallen for at that chance
encounter on the train. Her smile still had the capacity
to remind him of those carefree days before the
children came along, walking the beach at Newquay,
exploring Scotland on the motor-bike, that weekend in
Paris. It was just that now she was so predictable; why
did she keep wearing that crumpled purple cardigan?
And why did she persist in saying 'Merci beaucoup'
when she was as English as strawberries and cream?
What was the cliché people used? Yes, a marriage as
comfortable as a pair of old slippers.

There was a time when the children kept them young
and energetic, but now Susan was working in America

and Paul seemed to be having such a wonderful time at Exeter University that his home visits were few and far between.

Martin's career as an insurance inspector wasn't giving him the satisfaction it had when, tired of his deskbound job, he'd applied to go 'out on the road' as it was called. He had an area covering part of North London, and Martin's face was a familiar sight to the brokers he called on every week as he sought to attract new business for his employers.

Reps from other companies, whom he saw from time to time, didn't stay so long; they got on to the management ladder before they reached his age. He kidded himself that forty-nine didn't sound so bad, especially as he took a pride in his appearance, with his well-cut suit and his Abercrombie shirt. But in his heart of hearts, he knew he'd missed the boat. And he didn't care to think about that big number that lay round the corner.

However, there had come a ray of sunshine into his rather monochrome life, ever since, a couple of weeks ago, on making his regular call at the offices of Acme Insurance Agency, he was greeted by a new partner, a very attractive woman called Serena, whose mission seemed to be to add some zip to a rather tired set-up.

In contrast to the partners whom he'd known for years, with their usual banter about the respective fortunes of Spurs and Arsenal, Serena's conversation was lively and energetic. She looked to be in her mid-thirties, though Martin suspected she was a few years older. Gossip around the saloon bars had it that she was divorced and had taken up this senior position at a suburban broker's after working for one of the big-name city firms.

She certainly seemed to be on the ball... in more ways than one, thought Martin. And just yesterday, she had rung him to say that she had a large group life assurance scheme to place; why didn't they discuss it over lunch? Martin was only too pleased to agree, and it was easy to cancel his existing appointments.

'I must have made a hit with her' he'd thought as he chose his smartest shirt and most fashionable tie that morning. 'After all, she's probably 40; not much younger than 49.' He thought about his refined taste in reading and love of good music, and felt that he must be like a breath of fresh air to her after the dull men in her office, with their endless chatter about football. He allowed his mind to wander along paths rarely travelled as he thought of what it might lead to.

He'd chosen to introduce Serena to the Greyhound, a rather superior gastro-pub which he visited with important clients, and which he felt sure would not be used by Serena's colleagues at the Acme. He couldn't help feeling a quickening of his pulse as they both arrived exactly at twelve-thirty and she made a joke about punctuality. 'Mmm, she does look good,' thought Martin as he helped her off with her coat and she slipped off her scarf and gloves.

They were shown to the cosy corner table which he had taken the precaution of booking and settled into the comfortable chairs. What an excellent environment in which to develop a business relationship into something... well, something more intimate...

Serena picked up the menu and a glint of light caught Martin's eye. His heart sank as he allowed his eye to rest on a solitaire diamond ring on the third finger of her left hand. Serena's eye caught his with what just might have been a flash of amusement.

"Oh, you've noticed my ring. Isn't it a beauty! I know I should be thinking 'once bitten, twice shy' but this time will be for keeps. My partner Kurt took me to this wonderful restaurant in Covent Garden last Saturday and popped the question. He was so sure of my answer that he had the ring in his pocket." Martin gave the expected congratulations, though with a feeling that he'd never been more insincere.

As they were waiting for their meal to be served, Serena took a folder from her brief case and began to explain how this large sports and social club wanted to arrange a life assurance and personal accident cover for all its members.

"In the office, they said you were the best person to get this contract placed; apparently you're the oldest and most experienced of all the company reps."

Feeling 59 rather than 49, Martin read through the prospectus over an elegantly-presented meal.

Afterwards, Serena thanked Martin for the meal adding, with that delightful twinkle in her eye,

"Though I'm sure I should be thanking the Royal Standard Insurance Group!" Martin returned to the office with a sense of unfulfilled expectations.

He had to console himself with the thought of some substantial business coming his company's way as he sat in his usual armchair watching the dying embers of the open fire...

Martin's reflections on what might have been were interrupted by a plaintive cry from across the room.

"I'm stuck darling, can you help me out again? – Two words, 4 letters and 5 letters. Clue is: Wet Guy Fawkes night – what a let-down. Second letter of first word is A, so I think it must be 'rain.' The second word's got a Q in it so I may have something wrong."

Martin needed only a few seconds thinking time, then couldn't help giving a wry smile.

"The answer's pretty obvious, my dear – Damp Squib! He winced as the reply came from Betty in her crumpled purple cardigan: "Merci beaucoup, dear."

* * *

Noises in the Night   *Polly Paice*

There it was again, that faint noise like a baby crying.
It gave Elva a strange feeling of fear. Not fear of the
noise, but fear for whatever or whoever was making
that pitiful noise. She tried to sleep, after all she had
searched every night of the dark moon and still couldn't
find out where it was coming from.

Elva was a priestess in The Temple of the Skies. Her
skin was the colour of a lightly baked Coya bean. Her
long dark hair was plaited around her face and fell into
luscious curls down her back. She was beautiful, with
large dark eyes framed by long curled lashes, and lips
as red as the Arla flower which bloomed so abundantly
around the temple.

However, her face was almost obscured by the
priestess veil. She could only show her face when she
was alone, or in the company of other priestesses.

The next morning, she stood alone unveiled and
gazing out over the jungle covered mountains. She was
happy in the mountains, but this morning she had a
feeling of unease. As if she were searching for a long-
lost memory, ethereal, out of reach. It unsettled her,
she felt restless and sad, yearning for something
unattainable.

She barely heard the chimes until her handmaiden
came to summon her to devotion. After devotion it was
time to receive the gifts from the villagers. Each
morning, gifts of food and drink were offered to the
priestesses in exchange for blessings on the village and
prayers for good health and a good harvest.

This morning a mother brought her sick child to be
blessed before she took him to the medicine man. Elva
experienced such a wave of fear and sorrow that she
began to shake and her breath came in short gasps. She
became lightheaded and eventually collapsed at the

feet of the mother and child.

Strange voices floated into her consciousness. Visions of fighting and fire, sounds of screaming, a sense of terror and running away. The sound of a baby crying. All this and then the bliss of unconsciousness.

* * *

Elva woke to the soothing sound of voices joined together in devotions. She was lying on a bed of soft animal fur. She gave thanks to the Manditex, a luxurious brother beast for his fur, and slowly opened her eyes. The priestesses were gathered before her, and even the High or Mother priestess was present. The high priestess ended the devotion and dismissed the priestesses.

"How are you child?" enquired the high priestess softly. "You gave everyone a fright, are you feeling better now?"

"I don't know" replied Elva, "It was so strange, I felt such fear and sadness when I saw the sick child, and such strange and disturbing visions, what's wrong with me?"

"We will talk later child, but now you must eat and drink. You have been away from us for two days now. I will ask a handmaiden to prepare a meal for you, then you must rest. I will visit you after evening devotion, we will talk then." Elva lay there, what does it all mean, she thought, I can't eat a thing I'm too confused.

However, when the handmaiden came with a delicious platter of fragrant vegetables, luscious fruits and crisp flatbreads, Elva began to feel hungry and before long she had eaten it all. The young girl returned.

"The mother asked me to give you this and to tell you to drink it all." Elva thanked the girl and began to drink the amber liquid. It tasted sweet and strong. Her mouth began to fizz, but being obedient she drank it all. Gradually a feeling of well-being spread through her body and she slept, this time a deep, peaceful sleep.

She woke to the sound of bells calling her to devotion.

"The venerable priestess has said you are excused devotion this evening," said the young girl. "I will assist you to wash and change your gown for her visit later." Refreshed and with clean robes, Elva awaited the High Priestess's visit.

Elva arose and bowed before the High Priestess.

"No need to bow to me today, I have much to say to you. Sit, and tell me of your worries and your visions." Elva sat and told the Mother of hearing noises in the night like an infant crying, and of searching, during the time of the dark moon.

"The dark moon is a strange time," said the Mother, "tell me what happened when you went to bless the sick infant?"

"I don't know, I only know that I felt so sad," breathed Elva; she went on to describe her vision of fighting and fire, fear and running.

"My child, I have something to tell you and you must listen until the end" said the High Priestess softly, her eyes filling with tears. Elva was now sorely afraid of what was to come; she had never seen the High Priestess cry. "What do you remember of the time before you came here?"

"Nothing, I thought I've always been here, please tell me," cried Elva, now truly alarmed. The Priestess began.

"Many phases of the moon ago, you were found wandering in the jungle rambling and afraid, carrying a dead infant in your arms. You refused to part with him and became wild and incoherent. We had to sedate you in order to relieve you of the child who had been deceased for many days." Elva cried out in alarm and began to cry. The High Priestess continued, "We tried for days to find out who you were and what had happened to you, but your distress was so great that we worried for your sanity. You were wailing for your child both day and night, and we made the difficult decision to invoke the 'mind of the gods' to give you back your sanity and peace of mind. It was the only way. We used the serum of truth and memory to ascertain what had happened to you, then invoked the mind of the gods to help you forget."

"I will finish your tale, and then you can ask me any questions you want. You were born in a village beyond the mountains and lived there happily as a child and young woman. You were married and had a boy child. Your husband was a kind and gentle soul, but was trained in the martial-arts of combat.

"One day word began to reach your village of vicious invaders from the north, with flaming red hair and piercing green eyes. One by one the villagers fled before them. They were rumoured to have a dragon which was thought to be a magical beast. Each transit of the moon brought more people who had fled from the invaders to your village. On the third dark moon the nearest villagers arrived, along with survivors from more distant villages.

"Your husband, who was trained as a warrior said, 'We cannot run away anymore; we live on the edge of the dark jungle and we can't survive in there. We are many now, we must stand and fight. We need a group to lead them away into the dark jungle, I know a path on the edge, I can lead them deeper into the dark jungle where they will never survive. It is the dark moon, so we have the advantage.' And so, they stayed, women and children hid in caves and the brave villagers stayed to face the flame-haired invaders."

"The invaders came and they did indeed have a dragon or a machine that spewed fire. Your villagers fought bravely while others fled into the surrounding jungle. The invaders slaughtered many brave men and destroyed the village with their fire. The remaining men fled into the jungle.

"The invaders then set-about looking for women and children. Many were slaughtered, but the young women were spared for the invaders' entertainment. You were still suckling your baby and you begged for him to be spared if you cooperated willingly. The leader liked the look of you and said he would spare the brat if you would be his woman."

"You endured this humiliation for many days, but your baby was fretful and one night the leader beat him savagely to make him be quiet. In a fit of rage, which gave you strength, you attacked the leader with his own sword and fled into the dark jungle with your injured child. The leader was so enraged that he ordered his men into the dark jungle in pursuit."

"It is not known how you survived, but many of the pursuing invaders did not. For many days you roamed with your then dead infant, calling for your husband. You were found by some of the survivors of the carnage, wandering at the edge of the dark jungle babbling and incoherent, trying to suckle your dead child and refusing to give him up to anyone."

"It was decided to ask for our help, but we live on the other side of the dark forest. A brave survivor volunteered to guide you through the secret paths of the dark jungle, and by the will of the gods you both survived the journey."

"They brought you to us as you were the wife of the dead martyr who stopped the invaders. But my child, it was you who led the invaders into the dark jungle and to their deaths."

"We took you in and cared for you, but you still refused to give up your dead child. We decided that the only way we could help you was to invoke the mind of the gods to give you back your sanity. To do that we had to take away your memories. Forgive us, it was the only way. However, your memories were strong and you are beginning to remember."

"Yannis... that was the name of my husband; and my little boy... what has become of them?" cried Elva.

"We have laid your child to rest according to our customs," replied the Mother Priestess, "he is at peace. Yannis was never found. Many believe he led the remainder of the invaders to the dark jungle. We may never know."

"I know" wailed Elva "I know because I saw him in

the jungle, he called my name and I ran, or I think I did; I'm not sure about anything anymore. What am I to do now?"

"We could do again what we have done" said the High Priestess, "but you are stronger now, I believe you could endure your memories now. But be aware, you may not want, or be able, to truly abide by our rules and become one of us again. It is your decision, take some time to decide. The villager, Antin, is the one who guided you to us; he knows the paths through the dark jungle, if you decide to return to your own village."

Elva asked to see where her child was laid and the High Priestess took her to his grave.

During the next few days Elva spent a lot of time beside her child's grave, and in conversation with Antin before she made her decision.

"There's nothing at my village for me now" explained Elva, "This is my home now, and this is where my child lays, I wish to stay, if I can remain as a priestess. I will truly try to still be a priestess, but with my memories intact."

"That is all we ask," replied the High Priestess. "We will take it day by day, and if you decide that the memories prevent you from your vocation you may remain with us as a Handmaiden."

And so it will be.

* * *

Diamond Wedding
Mike Gardiner

*Reflection on a Diamond Wedding Celebration for Sixty
which had to be cancelled, only to be replaced by an
Anniversary-day summons to jabs for two!*

Let me not to the marriage of true minds
Admit impediments. Indeed, wise bard,
T'were always thus, but global pestilence
Can thwart the best-laid plans of lovers true

To celebrate the coming of the day
That marked the sixty years since their young lives
Were bound for ever in that sacred tryst
Of lifelong fond devotion care and trust

For in those dreadful days of uncut locks
Spoke one whose hair had always looked untrimmed
Forbidding gatherings of more than six
And even then, in frost and winter wind

And so...
It was a day that was not meant to be.
Crisp invitations lay unwritten in the box,
The family not summoned from their homes
And distant relatives remained unbid

Just Write

The sixty who'd been meant to dine
On side of beef or leek and Stilton tart (v)
Whose allergies and choices would become
Part of the preparation of that day

Were spared the pressures of the motorway,
The anxious glance at watches – are we late?
The unfamiliar look of Sussex lanes
The wond'ring – Is the Satnav really right?

The struggle with those ill-remembered names,
The difficulty knowing who's with whom,
The cousin's cry of feigned surprise "Why Mike,
You haven't changed a bit" (he knows he lies)

And then when all was cancelled, tears were dried,
Grim Covid chose to deal the final blow,
An invitation! Not to celebrate,
But stand in Clair's doomed Hall and to be jabbed

Upon that very day of fond recall
O cruel chance – how could you be so mean,
Intruding on that blessed day of joy
With painful arm and nauseous side effects

But...
How true the bard's wise words: Love is not love
Which alters when it alteration finds,
And never plague nor pestilence can mar
That bless'd eternal union of true minds

* * *

10 Word Poem

Restless Legs Syndrome

By Polly Paice

Walking

Pain

Crying

Despair

More drugs

More walking

Dawn

REST

10 Word Poem

Storms
By Carol Merrett

Storms
Savagely
Striking
Sun-drenched
Streams.
Thunder
Teasingly
Torments
Thrashing
Torrents.

Too Late for the Party
Gordon Reece Davies

Audrey was in the kitchen, doing her best to remove a raspberry jelly from its mould without breaking it. Having pressed around the edges, she put a plate on top of it and turned it upside down, shaking vigorously until she heard the slurping noise which told her it had come free. She put it down on the kitchen table and carefully lifted the mould. In the background she could hear the squeals and laughter of her five-year old son's birthday party in full swing. She was glad her neighbour's teenage daughter had volunteered to help with the games. There was a knock at the door.

The caller was wearing a fur-lined flying jacket over the uniform of the US Army Air Force. A jeep was parked on the road outside. Audrey looked at the man in stunned silence for several seconds.

"Audrey, honey, it's me, Eddy," the airman leaned back and spread his arms, a huge grin on his face.

"Eddy, yes... what are you doing here?" Audrey was hesitant, distracted.

"Sorry, honey I should have written. I got shot down on D-day and they shipped me back to the States. I didn't know too much about it for some weeks... but I'm fine now. Finally managed to get myself posted to Lakenheath just a couple a miles down the road."

"Yes, but D-day was six years ago. They said you were missing in action. When I didn't hear from you, I thought you must be dead! The war's been over nearly five years. Things are different now. You can't just turn up like this." Audrey noticed a movement in the lace curtain of the house opposite.

"I know it's a bit of a shock, honey, but I still feel the same way about you." He removed his peaked cap and patted down his blond hair. "Ain't you going to ask me in? I'd forgotten how cold it is over here in February."

"I can't, it's my son's birthday party I've got a house full of five-year olds."

Audrey could see why she had fallen for this good-looking clean-cut American – so different from stocky little Alfie, the man she'd actually married. She'd known Alfie since schooldays and they had been engaged before his call-up as a stoker on merchant-navy ships. He'd been away for most of the war on the dangerous Russian convoys. Months on end of never knowing whether he was alive or dead had taken its toll on her.

It had seemed like a bit of light relief when her friend suggested she should join her for the Saturday dance at the airbase where she worked. It had been easy enough to agree to dance with this handsome airman... and then to slide into an illicit romance with him.

"Mum, mum, we've finished playing blind man's buff, can we have our tea now?" A fair-haired child was tugging at her sleeve. He wore grey shorts and a white shirt with a red badge emblazoned with a big white number five.

"In a minute, darling, Lootenant Miles was just going."

"It's Major now, but that don't matter. Say, is this the birthday boy?" He crouched down and extended a hand towards the boy.

"Pleased to meet ya, son, you can call me Eddy. Say, that's a real neat button you got there." He reached out and touched the boy's red badge.

"It's my birthday badge it says five. I'm five today." He took hold of the badge and thrust it proudly towards the airman.

"What's his name?" looking up at Audrey.

"Edward."

"Well, Edward, I sure wish you a happy birthday... bet they call you Eddy too, huh?"

"We call him Ted, for short," Audrey spoke sharply.

"OK, Ted, maybe I've got something for you."

The airman was reaching into his jacket to withdraw his pocket-book, from which he handed a ten-shilling note to Edward. Edward stared at the note. It was more money than he had ever held in his hand before. He looked up at his mother who nodded,

"What do you say?"

"Thank you, Eddy," mumbled the five-year old.

"You're welcome, son," said Eddy.

Edward ran off to join his friends, waving the note and shouting excitedly.

"You shouldn't call him that" Audrey looked at Eddy, "I have to get back to the party."

"But is he...?" Eddy had been working out the timings in his head but couldn't bring himself to say the words. He thought he detected half a nod from Audrey before she pushed him away.

"I'm sorry, you really must go! Edward's father will be home soon, and he mustn't find *you* here. Now go!"

Eddy turned and walked dejectedly towards the road. Audrey followed him.

"I'm really sorry, Eddy, but it's for the best. I don't want you coming back here, you need to leave us alone."

She watched as he started his jeep and drove away. In tears, she shut the gate behind him and went back to the party.

* * *

Mary Richard

I am a retired registered nurse and have lived in Sussex throughout my life. My family is large and complicated, with interesting stories to tell. When relating some of the stories to my children and trying to explain who came where and did what, they would urge me to write it down. We often wish we had asked our parents more questions about their childhood. So, with all that in mind and with more time to pursue such things, I am attempting to fulfil my children's wishes and 'write it down'!
Mary Richard

BOWER FARM
and
CHAILEY WW2 AIRFIELD
Mary Richard

Bower Farm

Bower Farm, lying between Chailey Common and
Plumpton Green, now occupies approximately 220
acres of land. It had been a farm of 100-110 acres for
many centuries. At the East Sussex Records Office it is
mentioned as early as 1296 when 'John at the Bure'
(The Bower) is recorded. In January 1811, The Bower

was sold to Sir Henry Poole and at that point became a part of the ancient Hooke Estate. The tithe map of 1840 shows evidence of an oast house and a mill and many of the field names listed remain in use today.

The original part of the farmhouse, two up, two down, is timber framed and dated before 1600. In Victorian times, between 1840 and 1873, the house was extended around the original building to become the substantial farmhouse it is today. The large fireplace of the main living area was originally thought to have been a 'smoke bay' with just an opening in the roof, before the existing large brick chimney was built. Either side of the hearth metal rings are embedded in the brickwork to hold fire irons. On the large wooden beam at the front of the house are what is believed to be witches' marks. In the large garden which surrounded the house were two wells, which up until the late forties/early fifties, provided water for the farmhouse. The grounds also had three ponds, only a few feet deep in water but several feet deep in soft treacherous mud. Very little survived in these ponds other than eels and frogs.

Bower Farm acreage was increased in the 1860s with the purchase of Westlands and Gurrs Farm. It is believed that Westlands originally belonged to Lewes Priory until the dissolution of the monasteries by Henry VIII. It is thought that he bequeathed the land to Anne of Cleves as part of her divorce settlement. An Elizabethan Manor house once stood on the land but was eventually demolished. It is likely that some of the materials, such as bricks and wooden beams, were used in the construction of the two pairs of farm cottages at Westlands and Gurrs Farm. Westlands was later converted into one dwelling.

* * *

Westlands (Chailey Airfield)

Westlands has its own special history. In 1942 the farm was requisitioned by the ministry to create a fighter station as part of the expansion of fighter command following the Battle of Britain. It was not laid out until 1943 by which time the strategy had changed and it passed to the 2nd Tactical Air Force  to become an operating station for the invasion of continental Europe, codenamed Operation Overlord.

According to the 1838 tithe map, the site used was originally three fields; Westlands Field, Rough Pasture and Bower Green, whose hedgerows were uprooted in 1943 to construct Chailey Advanced Landing Ground, a temporary airfield. Two runways were built, running north-south and east-west.

At the end of the planned runway stood two houses and a pub, The Plough Inn.

These were demolished by the RAF.

A temporary pub was set up in a Nissen hut. It was a long, single storey building in dark wood with the Public Bar at one end and the Saloon Bar at the opposite end. This building was rebuilt in 1956 as the brick building that stands today. A memorial in the grounds of the pub pays tribute to pilots, in particular to the two Polish airmen who lost their lives.

RAF Chailey hosted 131 Polish Wing, with three squadrons, as well as number 18 Fighter Section, controlling three wings of three squadrons, five of which were also Polish (302, 306, 308, 315 and 317) as well as squadrons from Mysore (129), Natal (222), Belgium (349) and New Zealand (485). The station's officer commanding was the highest-ranking Pole in the RAF, Group Captain Aleksander Gabszewicz.

Spitfire squadrons from Belgium and New Zealand were also based there.

* * *

The airfield was mothballed in 1945, and in 1947 sold off and returned to agricultural  use. Nearly all associated buildings were temporary except for the brick pump-house which was part of the fuel dump, and still stands today. This was all surrounded by high earth banks to protect the tanks and buildings from bomb blasts. All but a short section of these banks has since been levelled.

The airfield's headquarters were situated at Bower Farm whilst the officers' quarters were located at Westlands, Beresford Lane, which still retains the wartime whitewash around the door.

* * *

In August 2004 a commemorative air show was held over two days, when, once again World War II Spitfires flew over and landed at Westlands.

The following is an extract from a review of the air show, courtesy of Andrew Critchell, LRPS, Aviation photographer and historian. (aviationphoto.co.uk)

Chailey Air show – Bower Farm, East Sussex 7th and 8th August 2004

Review – For two days in August the lush farmland in East Sussex that, in 1944, had been the site of RAF Chailey Advanced Landing Ground, again resounded to the mighty roar of Rolls Royce Merlin engines as the Chailey 2004 Air show and Fly-in got underway. Held on Bower Farm, the show commemorated the exploits of the Spitfire-flying Polish airmen of 131 Wing.

The Polish 131 Wing, consisting of 302, 308 and 317 squadrons, flew Spitfire Mk.XIs from Chailey in support of Operation Overlord, the liberation of Europe, including flying four missions on D-Day itself. 131 Wing was commanded by Battle of Britain veteran Group Caption Aleksander Gabszewicz.

The link with Chailey, D-Day and 1944 also extended to three of the Spitfires in attendance.

The Historic Aircraft Collection's Mk.Vb BM597 was flown during 1942 and 1943 by various Polish pilots from 316 and 317 squadrons and is currently painted in the markings of 317 squadron.

The Old Flying Machine Company's Spitfire Mk.XI MH434 flew with 222 squadron on D-Day, part of 135 Wing which was also commanded by Group Captain Gabszewicz. For the show MH434 was painted in the personal markings of the Group Captain, including his famous boxer motif on the nose, and Ray Hanna closed the show with a typically scintillating display.

Carolyn Grace's Spitfire Mk.XI ML407 also flew on D-Day with 485 squadron, also part of 135 Wing, and both 222 and 485 squadrons were personally led by Group Captain Gabszewicz on a mission on 7th June 1944. The link with Poland was continued to the present day, as some veterans were able to attend the show and sit again inside the cockpit of a Spitfire.

The afternoon's flying was a delight for warbird fans with no less than four Spitfires (Breighton, N. Yorkshire, based PR.XI PL965 being the fourth), two

Hurricanes (Historic Aircraft Collections Mk.XII G-HURI alongside the Real Aeroplane Company's XII BE417/G-HURR).

Two P-51D Mustang's (Rob Davies 'Big Beautiful Doll' and Maurice Hammonds 'Janie') ...

('Janie')

...and The Fighter Collection's mighty P-47D Thunderbolt in attendance.

A good number of historic types attended the fly-in element of the show, including 1935 built Miles Hawk Speed Six G-ADGP and Hurn based Auster 5 RT486 / G-AJGJ resplendent in D-Day invasion stripes. The Aircraft Restoration Company's immaculate Harvard Mk.IV G-BGPB was also present in its Portuguese Air Force colours.

Our grateful thanks to Andrew Critchell L.R.P.S. for allowing this extract to be included.

The photos of aircraft were taken at the Chailey air show by Gordon Davies. All other photos from Mary's family album.

A book by Richard Whittle tells the story of the little-known airfield at Bower Farm, Chailey and its Polish Spitfire Squadrons - its title: 'Spit and Polish.'

* * *

David Gee

Married to Liz for 53 years, blessed with a son, daughter, and 5 grandchildren.

I was a director of a PLC developing and operating high dependency Nursing Homes specialising in care for the elderly mentally ill.

My passion is sailing – I have owned several yachts and competed in many offshore races. I like politics, philosophy, current affairs, and British military history. I formed a company that restored Fort Newhaven which is now in the care of Lewes District Council.

My writing has been reports and presentations. I am learning to write for pleasure, I find it therapeutic but only those subjects that interest me.

Louis Acott   *David Gee*

A Story of courage and service over two World Wars in the Royal Navy.

LOUIS FREDERICK HENRY ACOTT was born at Berkhamsted, Hertfordshire on 10th May 1896. He attended the local school and although not an academic lad, he was a well behaved and sociable boy. His family were not well off, and he had to leave school early to find paid work as a gardener's boy. Gardening, although enjoyable, was not a career option for him.

In August 1910 at the age of 14 he applied to the Royal Navy as a boy entrant. The Navy would not accept him for formal training until he was sixteen. In June 1912 he joined H.M.S. Ganges. The physically hard disciplined life as a boy entrant suited Louis and after his initial induction he signed up for a 12-year engagement.

His first ship was H.M.S. Crescent, an 'Edgar' class battle cruiser, which he joined in April 1913. The ship was attached to the Home Fleet, based in Scapa Flow, Scotland. The clouds of war were brooding as H.M.S. Crescent, together with her escorting destroyers, patrolled the North Sea.

Life was hard in the Royal Navy at that time, especially for boy sailors. Ships were coal-burning and coaling was very dirty and physically exhausting work. A Battle Cruiser on patrol would consume between 750 and 1,000 tons of coal in a week, or even more if sustained high speed was required. Coal had to be loaded in hundredweight sacks by hand into the ship's bunkers. In 1914, the Royal Navy had a fleet of 305 colliers each with a capacity of 3,000 tons of coal. They also had a further 18 colliers in reserve to meet their needs in the U.K. and around the world.

Louis' next ship was H.M.S Indefatigable, a

Dreadnaught class battleship, with a complement of 1,018 men. This ship was later lost in the Battle of Jutland on the first of May 1916 with only three survivors. During that terrible day more than 6,000 British sailors lost their lives, mainly in the three ships H.M.S. Invincible, H.M.S. Queen Mary, and H.M.S. Indefatigable, due to direct hits on their magazines. This triggered catastrophic explosions. Louis was fortunate not to be aboard the Indefatigable at that time. He had been transferred to H.M.S. Hind, a Destroyer, and later, to H.M.S. Apollo, a light Cruiser, in which he saw action throughout the 1914-18 war, surviving several engagements.

After the First World War he married Sarah Anne Broome. They had two daughters: Gwen, in 1919 and Patricia, in 1921.

Louis rose through the ranks to become a petty officer. He loved the Royal Navy, the comradeship, and the ability to travel the world. The drawback was being separated from his wife and children for extended periods, usually six to nine months at a time.

From 1918, until 1936, he served on a series of ships that have subsequently become Royal Naval folklore such as H.M.S. Valiant (battleship), H.M.S. Resolution (battleship) and H.M.S. Hood, a battle cruiser (subsequently lost with 1,500 crew in 1941 in the Denmark Straights when a shell from the Bismarck caused yet another catastrophic explosion in one of her magazines). Louis also served on H.M.S. Eagle (aircraft carrier), H.M.S. Argus (aircraft carrier), H.M.S. Queen Elizabeth (battleship) and several destroyers. He travelled the world serving on the China station (Hong Kong), the South Africa station (Simonstown), Malta and Gibraltar. There were few major ports in the world he did not visit. He was paid-off in May 1936 and went to work in a relative's wine business in Leicester.

1938 saw Louis recalled by the Royal Navy. He was promoted to chief petty officer and served on H.M.S. Drake as a gunnery instructor. In March 1941 he joined H.M.S. Exeter, a York class Cruiser. Exeter had just undergone a major two-year refit at Devonport dockyard, following the extensive battle damage sustained in December 1939 during the battle of the River Plate, with the German pocket battleship Graf Spee. Exeter's refit was hurriedly completed, and she was despatched to the Pacific following the loss of H.M.S. Prince of Wales, and H.M.S. Repulse.

Exeter was in constant action for the next eleven months protecting convoys and shelling Japanese installations as the Japanese relentlessly advanced through the Pacific towards Australia. She was the last capital warship to leave Singapore, having to hurriedly cut the fuel lines and blow up the fuel depot whilst under heavy fire from the invading Japanese. Her crew were blooded and worn out from being in continual action and consistently under aerial attacks.

On 27th February 1942, during the first battle of the Java Sea, Exeter sustained serious battle damage when a Japanese 8-inch shell penetrated one of her engine rooms, killing fourteen of her crew and wounding another ten. This substantially reduced her speed and ability to manoeuvre. Her engineers managed to carry out emergency repairs, but Exeter had to go into action again a few days later on the 1st March in the second battle of the Java Sea in the Saundra Straights.

Exeter was hopelessly outgunned against five Japanese cruisers and a destroyer flotilla. After a lengthy engagement she sustained yet another 8-inch shell in her engine room and lost all propulsion and electric power. She was dead in the water, sinking, unable to bring her gun turrets to bear. Enemy shells were raining down on her and several fires raged out of control as oil lines ignited. Sea cocks were opened to ensure her hulk did not fall into Japanese hands, and the order to abandon ship was issued. Her escorting destroyers, H.M.S. Encounter and the American destroyer, U.S.S. Pope were also lost in this engagement.

During the action, Louis's gun turret received a direct hit from a Japanese 8-inch shell, killing most of the gun crew. Louis had his leg severely injured by shell splinters. He spent the next 27 hours swimming in shark infested waters before being picked up by a Japanese destroyer.

He was taken to Mocassar in the south-west of the Island of Celebes, now called Sulawesi. On arrival, prisoners were forced to march in the tropical heat through the town to demonstrate to the local population the superiority of the victorious Japanese. Very few had shoes and many could barely stand. Louis's injured leg had turned septic. His leg and life were saved a few days later in the camp by a fellow prisoner, a medic, who operated on him with no anaesthetic, only a razor blade and a sewing kit. Conditions in the camp were shocking, with 90 men allocated to a bamboo hut. Louis endured three and a half years of forced labour, brutality, starvation, and disease. Only 200 of Exeter's 650 complement survived the sinking and the Japanese internment. They were eventually repatriated when the Islands were liberated by the Americans in 1945.

The survivors were transported to Darwin Australia on H.M.S. Maidstone. Louis remained there in hospital for six months before he was strong enough to be shipped back to the U.K. He said he would never forget the kindness, care and affection shown to him by the nurses and people of Darwin and he considered they saved his life. His normal weight was fifteen and a half stone. On arrival in Australia, he weighed five stone nine pounds. Constant beating, malnutrition, and tropical diseases had done irreparable damage to his optic nerve and he was permanently blinded. He was covered with scars and had sustained nine broken bones and innumerable fractures.

The Japanese did not pass on any information about the prisoners to the Allies. Louis' wife Sarah was told he was missing in action presumed dead and for three years she received a war widows' pension. Not once in that time did Sarah doubt Louis would one day return home.

In the camp, Louis did his best to maintain discipline, instilling in the men the belief that somehow, they would survive and return home. This indomitable spirit, without doubt, saved lives. On repatriation he brought out with him a faded list of names he had kept hidden from the Japanese during incarceration. Had he have been caught with this he would have been beheaded. He had recorded the names, dates, and causes of death of his fellow prisoners that died in captivity on the basis that their families would want this information, and as a record of Japanese brutality.

Louis arrived back in England and was reunited with his wife and daughters on 27th February 1946. Sarah and he went to live with their oldest daughter Gwen, her husband and their new-born son in their Public House at Greenhithe Kent.

During the next few years, Louis regained his strength thanks to Sarah's love and care, but he was unable to recover his eyesight. He still suffered occasional nightmares and the after-effects of malaria, and beri-beri. He did however, have an iron constitution and maintained his indomitable spirit.

He had little time for the lazy, feckless, dishonest or disrespectful. He believed that life required discipline and rules to live by. Sometimes this irritability showed publicly, and he was thought by some to be stubborn and cantankerous. He was careful with his money, believing in independence. He was a great supporter of punctuality and his mantra was 'If you did not arrive for an appointment five minutes early, you were late, and being late was a discourtesy.' He was also convinced there was nothing finer than being British, and that that total loyalty to his country and family was essential to civilised society. In summary he was Royal Navy, principled and disciplined through and through.

Louis showed no irritability with his young grandson. They spent many hours together. The boy was proud to be with him. They became remarkably close. They listened to talking books, gardened, went fishing together. During school holidays with Sarah, they would stay at Seasalter near Whitstable where the family had a small holiday bungalow on the beach.

The boy would guide Louis every day when they went out for walks and describe the scene to him as they walked. When, later, the boy came of age, he would take Louis out regularly first as a pillion passenger on his motor scooter, usually to the pub. Later he would take him in a car that Louis had helped him fund, and which the boy paid him back in full. They enjoyed each other's company. Louis told him about his life in the Navy and the ports he had visited. He was a major influence in the boy's life. He taught him independence and to stand up for himself as well as many other life skills, not least to splice ropes and rove wire before the boy was ten. At no time did Louis ever discuss his time as a P.O.W., but he hated rice and all Japanese manufactured products.

Louis suffered a stroke in November 1975 from which he recovered. He had a second stroke seven months later in June 1976 and passed away peacefully at his home to join his shipmates at the age of 79. Sarah and his family, including his grandson were by his side. He bequeathed his medals, service records and life principles to his grandson who keeps them with pride and will pass them on to his son and daughter, and in turn hopes they will be passed on to his grandchildren.

As you may have guessed I am Louis's grandson, and to this day I consider myself privileged to have had such a fine man for my grandfather. I will always be grateful to have been able to spend my formative years in his company. I remain in awe of his courage, fortitude, standards and record of service to his country.

* * *

Out Manoeuvred   *Mary Richard*

The shrill bell brought them instantly awake. There was no time for delay as they dragged their aching bodies from a dreamless sleep, induced after yesterday's long and grueling exercises over rough terrain. The grey dawn signaled yet another wet, miserable day and the prospect of more demanding manoeuvres. Today it was the obstacle course.

Harry stared gloomily at the large area of netting stretched over the wet, sticky black mud. With gritted teeth and a determined scowl, he adjusted his rucksack, belt and gun and waited for the signal. On cue he dropped to his knees and started scrambling under the net, his gun dragging and catching on the rough ground.

The next he knew there was a loud sharp crack and then a searing pain as a bullet ripped into his forearm. He had somehow released the safety catch and his body movement over the ground had triggered the gun.

As he lay there a thought crossed his weary mind; there would be no more manoeuvres for him for a while.

A small, wry smile crossed his lips as his colleagues rushed to his aid.

* * *

A Passing Phase   *Carol Merrett*

Pulsating, pushing, throbbing, the tiny shoot emerges victorious;

Breathing pure spring air, twisting its head in the bellows of virgin breezes.

Life begins spontaneously,

But never stops moving on the gently swirling wheel of life.

Shoots grow, flowers emerge, buds burgeon, bursting their skins,

Growing, learning hour by hour.

A mirror of our own lives... babies burst from the womb, wailing lungs, flailing limbs.

Growing, learning hour by hour.

Days lengthen, shoots thrive, limbs extend as summer approaches.

Babies, blossoms, bask in the sunlight yearning,

Seeking the sunshine with thirsty mouths;

Tongues lapping, limbs twisting, turning like an eel writhing in the shallows.

Laughter caresses and love excites, joy throbs exultantly,

Pulsating like a rocket exploding in the cosmic sky!

A time of movement, excitement, progress, never standing still.

Growing, learning hour by hour.

The glowing orb of life-giving sun begins to wane,

Days shorten unperceived;

Tiredness contentedly invades every moving branch, every blade of gleaming grass.

Autumn percolates slowly with golden warmth,

Stretching our limbs, finding peace.

A sudden burst of energy, a spark of fire, a songbird's soaring flight of passion,

Breezes powerfully energising the swirl of life.

Growing, flowing, learning hour by hour.

Listen, watch as winter lays her seductive mantle around the world;

Like a mother embracing her children,

Gently shielding them from the frosts of the earth.

Leaves tumble, plants curl up, birds flee to some mysterious heavenly kingdom.

What of us, people of experience, of wisdom, of life?

We have sprung into life, grown, learned, loved;

Burst into bud, flowered, withered, now sleeping, a smile creasing our faces.

Growing, slowing, learning hour by hour, year by year.

Dear Reader, can you not see, can you not learn?

How can we be so blind...?

Our lives are seasons, constantly moving, never standing still.

Like flowers, we push through the earth, we bud, we flower, we wilt until...

Reaching the winter of our life, we rest eternally in the arms of God.

* * *

After the Storm   *Hazel Lintott*

From the crest of the old mill bridge I can watch
　　The river in spate from yesterday's storm.
　　I feel the rumble and thund'ring of water,
　　　The power of the flood rushing by.
　　Branches are captured in giddying eddies
　　Islands of reeds swirl round unrelentingly
　　　Dancing a waltz on turbulent seas.
　　　Tumbling flotsam and foaming crests
　　Wallow and bellow in writhing impatience
　　To squeeze through the narrow and ferny arch.

As I lean on the bridge I can feel its bones shaking,
Place my hand on its lichen-clad brick as it braces
　Itself 'gainst a storm-laden flood that is racing
　　Through time-moulded archway beneath.

　　Out of the cavern spins a white feather
　　Surfing fast on the current to places beyond.
　　An old split paling, grabbed by the torrent,
　Seeks a moment of rest in some reeds by the bank,
Then caught by the tide it's dragged back on its journey
　　To carry on swirling and pitching and rolling
　　Until it is shattered and splintered and wrecked.
　　The ducks have deserted to swim on the millpond,
　　Terns dance in the wind in a graceful display
　　Now storm clouds are scattered and blowing away.

I breathe in the earthy-damp riverine mist
Rising up to the bridge from the tumult below;
Beneath me is thunder, upheaval and chaos
But I stand firm on the old cobbled road.

* * *

10 WORDS

Rose Garden
By Gordon Reece Davies

Dug the ground.
Planted, manured then pruned.
'What lovely roses!'

* * *

Sizzling Summer   *Norma Hall*

It didn't end up like it started, that dazzling, sizzling
Summer. To begin with, we were between two
sparkling expanses of water. On a strip of land
between the turquoise and silver lagoon of the Mar
Menor in Spain and the deeper blue luxurious
Mediterranean on the other side. Spoilt for choice,
we meandered between them, the 500 metres from
our holiday apartment on one side and then, maybe
the next day, or in the afternoon, about the same
distance on the other.

In the late afternoon, it was best to wander
down to the lagoon and idly watch the kite surfers
catching the wind and swooping down and around
the long stretch of the water, while we waited for the
increasingly silver and gold shimmers on the water
as the sun went slowly down. A little kiosk on the
sand sold beer and cacahuetes (Spanish peanuts),
and if it became more windy, gave shelter and a good
place to sit and watch; those long unhurried
evenings when time was always on our side.

But in the early morning, it was also the side to
take long walks along the shoreline, past the boats
with their differing lengths of masts silhouetted
against the skyline and the surrounding hills. There,
the mussel collectors could be seen between the
small peninsular and other inlets; knee deep in the
water, bending down collecting and filling the
pouches strapped to their trouser legs. Fishermen
worked on their boats in the dry dock along the way
and an old empty beach bar, with deserted wooden
benches and crooked umbrellas illustrated that
there was still much work to be done before the real
season began.

Swimming was best on the Mediterranean side,
which also had the best beach for sunbathing and
people watching. By mid-morning, the white sand
was warm and the sun hot on our increasingly
sunburned shoulders. Just right to make the short

stroll to the sea edge and slowly get used to the first cold shock of the waves, before plunging under and splashing away, legs kicking furiously. Once used to the temperature, you could float lazily on your back and watch the clouds scooting overhead. Heaven!

Families started to come down after that. First a father, helping his two small children with their buckets and spades, while mum had a rest further up the beach. Then a young couple, happy to use the water as a good excuse to get up close and personal, exchange a few hugs and kisses, their laughter ringing out across the wide horizon. People of all shapes, ages and sizes starting to promenade along the beach, a few dogs excitedly running and sniffing everywhere.

And so, onwards with the hire car journey, the exploration continued from old Cartegena, Bolnuevo beach with its ancient sandstone sculptures as big and craggy as small mountains, through the old Ports and larger towns. Almeria, the wondrous Granada with its Moorish Alhambra, Nerja and onto our final destination: Malaga, happily still out of season, with its purply blue jacarandas and bright reddish-purple bougainvillea, reminding us very much of our old home in Africa.

Summers always end, and paradise, like a crumpled bit of paper, has a strange way of slowly folding more reality into its creases. I knew it first the day I entered the water only to see hundreds of small jelly fish which halted my progress and, turning back, noticed children with small pointed fingers drawing their adults' attention to what was happening. They hastened from under umbrellas where they had been eating barbequed sardines from numerous small restaurants on the beach. Soon the waters had emptied and the trend continued further up the coast even to Fuengirola, when the first shark seen off a Mediterranean beach in decades, was spotted the day before we arrived.

The atmosphere seemed different too. I

watched as a small boy, excited and wanting to get into the water with the older children, could only hover anxiously until taken underarm by an older boy and dropped in the sea. Realising he couldn't swim and was nearly drowning, I leapt up, arms waving and was about to jump in, when a large angry mother eventually surfaced and swept him away with a scolding smack.

Further away we began to read of tragic fires in Greece claiming many lives, closely followed by those in Portugal and California. Worst ever, the headlines read and then the unprecedented heat waves in Europe, UK and much further afield: India, Japan and Australia, again with heavy costs for human and animal life and livelihoods.

Back home, we started-off enjoying that sizzling summer but by the time our South African relatives visited, eager to find the green gardens of England, there were only bleached landscapes and brown parks which reminded them of the dry plains and bushveld they had left behind them. Our country walks increasingly devoid of birds and wildlife.

With the build-up of heat, the inevitable storms, thunder and rains would eventually follow. We stared aghast as the television showed waters rising, rivers overflowing and bridges and buildings collapsing: the tragic bridge collapse in Italy, France where campers were washed away and left clinging to trees, Hawaii, Japan, Indonesia, India and all over. It seemed nowhere was to be spared entirely.

Yes, it didn't end up like it started, that sizzling summer, and though rain followed, it seemed more like a portent that things would no longer just return to normal. Change was both brooding and imminent, just below the surface waiting to catapult us all to a new more dangerous era.

* * *

10 Words

A Long Story
By Mike Gardiner -

In the beginning...Telescope to microscope.
Fourteen billion years... coronavirus!

***

The Painting   *Polly Paice*

It was a beautiful painting. We discovered it in the eaves of our new home. We moved into the lovely stone cottage a month ago. It was originally a crofter's home, nestling under a mountain in the Scottish Highlands. It had been extended and altered inside to a modern standard, but still kept the character with its sloping thatched roof. A low stone wall surrounded our small quaint garden, although the shadow of the mountain crept down all too soon. Nestled in the protection of the stone walls, the roses grew surprisingly well. There was also an abundance of yellow lilies, and a small vegetable patch.

In the painting, in this garden, stood a young woman of tender years. With long auburn hair blowing in the breeze, cheeks a delicate rosy hue, and lips as red as the setting sun, her large green eyes peered shyly but seductively from under long dark lashes. A purple and green tartan shawl was thrown casually around her slender shoulders; and underneath, a white gypsy blouse was low enough to give a glimpse of her young bosom. Behind her was the low stone wall, and beyond that glowed the purple heather and the burnished gold of the dying bracken. The sun slanted through dark clouds and seemed to bathe her in its soft golden light. It was obviously a picture painted with pure love.

I was intrigued with it, but my husband... well, he was mesmerised by it. He insisted on putting it in his study; I must admit I was a little jealous. He became obsessed with the painting, spending hours gazing at it. Even his work was suffering, but he blamed it on the somewhat spasmodic internet connection which he needed for his work.

Who was she? When was it painted? I longed to know. I made it my mission to find out more. I began at the local library, foraging in the archives, but to no avail. Wondering where to go next, I started to talk to the locals. Many were newcomers like us, but then I began to talk to older folk who had families going back generations. Finally, I found an old crofter, his face was wrinkled with age, and his body was bent from the harsh life he had led, but his tired eyes still twinkled. He remembered a tale told to him as a child.

In the house we now occupied lived a widowed crofter who had a beautiful young daughter. He was very protective of her and kept her close; but one summer a young Englishman named James Hammond wandered through the valley with his easel and paints; he was a handsome young man with dark curly hair and soft chocolate eyes.

James was a rich young man who painted for his leisure, and was particularly drawn to the magnificent landscapes of the Highlands. One morning, he spotted the young lass picking flowers for her father, and he was smitten. He melted into her large green eyes and longed to kiss her red lips. They met clandestinely each day, as her father would not have approved.

They walked over the purple heather and paddled in the bubbling stream. Some days they would climb a way up the mountain and sit gazing out over the valley. They fell in love, and James asked if he could paint her picture. She agreed, but said,

"I canna take it to mi home as mi da would not approve."

James started on the painting in a place where the willows grew; it would be more private there. He was about to finish the painting on the day he possessed her. The lassie was so ashamed at what she had done that she ran from him. James knew he had to finish the painting and began making the final touches to her seductive face. James was distraught, he knew he had done wrong and disgraced the young lass.

At the croft, her father could sense his daughter's agitation, but could get no answer from her. James haunted the places they went, but there was no sign of the lass, until one day he spotted her with a basket, foraging for berries. He went to her and begged for another chance.

"I canna" she said, "Mi da knows something is wrong. He watches me like the hawks that fly above." James was heartbroken, but realised that they could not meet again.

"But please take my painting of you," he pleaded. "I can paint another one for me." Finally, she relented and once they had said their tearful goodbyes, she wrapped the painting up in her shawl and ran back to the croft.

A few months went by, and the young lass realised that she was wi' bairn. She was weeping in her room looking at the picture when her father came in. Her father was no fool, he could see the changes in his daughter, and suspected that she may be wi' bairn. He snatched the painting

"So, this is the culprit," he cried in rage, "look at this painting, have you no shame?"

"Please let me have the painting," said the daughter, taking it from her father. Her father was enraged and took out his Dirk.

"I'll destroy it!" he roared, and lunged at the painting, intending to slash it to pieces. But the young lass moved to protect it, and her father's Dirk pierced her chest, mortally wounding her. The father was distraught, and vowed to find the young painter and kill him. He searched the neighbouring villages, but to no avail; the young painter had moved on.

The father admitted his crime to the authorities and was charged with manslaughter; but after hearing his story and seeing his obvious distress, the charge was dropped to accidental manslaughter. The judge ruled that the remorse and distress that the father would have to bear for the rest of his life was punishment enough, and he was released.

Back at the croft, the father could not bear to look at the painting, but he could not destroy it, as it was his only memory of his daughter. So he hid it under the eaves of the cottage, under the thatch; and there it remained until we found it.

But what of the young painter? Well, he went on to gain quite a reputation and did paint another picture of the young lass. After a lot of searching, I found out that this very painting was on display in the museum in Aberdeen, along with many of James' landscapes of the Scottish Highlands. It was a long journey, but, soon after, I managed to get to the city, and went to view the painting in the museum. However, there was one difference in that painting. Behind her stood a shadowy figure of a man with curly brown hair and smiling eyes. That man was of course, James Hammond.

In case you were asking, yes, I did tell my husband about the story behind the painting and suggested that we donate our painting to our local museum. After some persuading, he agreed. But I didn't tell him the thing that made shivers run down my spine that day in Aberdeen. The fact that the figure of James in the painting was the image of my husband, James Hammond.

* * *

Standing in the Field
Carol Merrett

I have returned.

Alone in a field of silence, I closed my eyes, inhaling deeply the perfume of my past.

The field of my youth lying seductively before me, enticing me into a meadow of memories.

Signs... Keep Out... Forbidden... Barbed wire... Anger

Returning in the autumn of my years to the autumn of my dreams

OUR field, once so beautiful in its simplicity, its purity

Its intoxicating power still enthralled me, still empowered me, still entrapped me.

Rustling... A sleek red fox... Powerful... Alert... Curious... Pungent.

I wept, silent tears rolling into the wrinkles, the saltiness wetting my crusty lips,

My childhood flashed vividly before me

Swishing, long, scratchy grass tickling my skinny legs,

Inhaling, the sweet-scented hay filling my lungs and mouth

Chasing, playing, giggling, carefree

Scudding clouds flying through an eternally azure sky

A buzzard hovering greedily over its innocent prey.

/Over

Tractors churning up the field... Mice scurrying in fright... Noise polluting my aged mind.

Why had I departed?

Why had I returned?

Nothing remains the same.

The wild freedom, the bubbling joy, the dizzy giddiness,

Three friends skipping, tumbling, fighting, wading through muddy streams

Running through swathes of wild, waving grass

Chasing elusive, crazy rabbits

Catching wriggling, squirming tadpoles.

The check-shirted farmer shouting at us, raising his fist, red-faced, breathless,

Us hiding, laughing, climbing ancient trees, building secret dens

Scraping knees, grazing elbows, grubby urchins.

Oozing mud... Scratches... Shouts... Escape... Run... Fall... Hide... Sweet grass.

Visions of an old man... I shake my balding head, open my bloodshot eyes,

Clouds of nostalgia coursing erratically through me, shaking the core of my being.

Fences... Restrictions... Do Not... Building... People... Chaos...

The trees have almost gone, fences encircle the field, a building site emerges,

People everywhere, noise, machines, noise, 'phones, noise... call it progress, a modern beauty.

A world that does not belong to me, a field that no longer belongs to me,

I bid OUR field farewell leaving the memories buried beneath its muddy furrows,

Laughter buried under the trees,

Dreams lifted up into the heavens

To shine on those who follow me.

Love... beauty... sunlight... happiness

* * *

Watching Boris – *Richard Hughes*

Watching Boris having neater hair by tiny, tiny increments
At each and every lectern show.
Growing my hair till it begins to flow.
Becoming comfortable in a new bed.
Thinking, always thinking
Instead of acting
Thinking, inventing patentable thoughts.

These days when Tuesday becomes another Tuesday
Without apparent or memorable event,
I feel a lack of urgency.
Days lost, as by an opium smoker
Except there has been no stumble back to sunlight
When the shilling has been smoked
And another idiot takes space by the oil lamp in the Opium Den.

Things that could be done include:
    Making talismans to stick pins in
    Draw plans for Xanadu mark two
    Cut a hedge because the chicks have fledged
    Visit Pub gardens with friends
    Renew memberships and join in again
But brooding suits me best.

The span of time, the elapse between cave painting
And Space walking
When chasing game and browsing forest and heath
for dinner
Long before there was a word for lunch
Lying around
Or weaving a handy pouch
Until the enclosure of animals, gathering and sorting
seeds began.

It may be that indolence,
Acting only as one pleased, was what each of us could
do.
Not only Lord Snooty and his crew
But perhaps we had time
Between feeds to laze about, dream
Create Castles in mid air
But low, look yonder.

I see myself approach.
And I'm waving a metaphorical pension book.
It's me who can be free from obligations that plague
the other folks.
I need not worry so
Not quite so much, perhaps, just mask up and do a bit
of shopping
Go to the dump
Of course, write poems, maybe a bunch.

* * *

Summer Rain
Hazel Lintott

Gradually the evening darkens
After such a sultry day.
"Storm's approaching" husband mutters
As gardening tools are put away.

Big raindrops fall on the decking
Spotting down with sharp pit-pat,
Neighbours close their windows quickly,
Indoors slinks the dampened cat.

Now the steady shower quickens,
Lower drops the darkening sky
Till the clouds embrace the hill tops
And revive an earth parched dry.

Wilting flowers raise their faces
To receive the gift bestowed;
Sheltering birds at roost in hedges
Feel the cooling breezes blow.

All across the gardens misting
Drives the summer rain so fresh.
Petals are dashed down to litter
On the pathways, shiny wet.

Safe and dry inside our houses,
Kettle on to make a brew,
We wait and watch and thank the heavens
For this reviving interlude.

* * *

Collateral Damage   *Mike Gardiner*

It was late afternoon on a day that had slipped out of mid-November and found its way to early April, causing people to make gloomy predictions about the Easter weather. The persistent light drizzle throughout the day had given way to a dank curtain of mist that clung to the plane trees around Trafalgar Square.

Sharon was in a gaggle of phlegmatically-resigned office workers waiting drably at the bus stop in Charing Cross Road. She searched the gloom in vain for any sign of the long-overdue number 29 that would take her home to Wood Green.

The tube from Leicester Square would have been much quicker, but never again would she travel on the Underground since the horrific experience of the previous July when her Piccadilly Line train had been torn apart by a terrorist bomb near Russell Square. She counted herself lucky to have been at the rear of the train, but had vowed to stick to buses in future.

Sharon fidgeted with impatience. Gerry was planning a special meal tonight to celebrate the first anniversary of his moving-in. The evening was going to be spoiled, and all because she'd had to stay late in the office to clear up that careless error she'd made earlier. A black cab was waiting in the stationary queue of traffic just five feet from her. The sign showed 'For Hire' and, on a sudden impulse, she caught the driver's eye and opened the passenger door.

"Bloody awful night tonight, my love. Where to?" came the voice of the cabbie as Sharon settled in her seat. His voice had a faint guttural tinge, possibly South African Sharon thought, though she was no judge of accents. She agreed with his assessment of the unseasonable weather, and asked him to take her to Mayes Road Wood Green.

"Number 152, just past the Library." After a moment's silence, as they edged closer to the traffic lights, the cabbie muttered,

"Strange, that, how long you've lived there?"

"Must be about five years now," ventured Sharon cautiously. "Why do you ask?"

"Oh, just making conversation," returned the driver. "Going away this year my love?"

The conversation drifted along desultory channels as the cab stopped and started its way through Tottenham Court Road and into Holloway. Sharon couldn't stop thinking about the cabbie's reaction to her living in number 152. She began to hear sinister undertones to his voice. She couldn't help wishing that the traffic would suddenly clear and that they could cover the remaining two or three miles in the fifteen minutes it would take, were it not rush hour.

It was all coming back to her. The reason that she'd been able to afford a roomy two-bedroomed apartment over a smart men's outfitters, was that it had been on the market for more than a year and the price had been knocked down several times. 152 Mayes Road was being spoken of in the same tones as 10 Rillington Place and 39 Hilldrop Crescent, because of what the papers had dubbed 'The Millennium Murder' and gawpers frequently stopped on the other side of the road to stare.

Sharon only plucked up the courage to buy it because a girlfriend was also looking for accommodation and asked if she could move in with Sharon as a paying tenant, which would mean that Sharon would not be alone in the flat and would be a useful help towards paying the mortgage.

A childless couple from South Africa had been living at no 152 for a few years. He was a quantity surveyor, she an ophthalmic nurse at Moorfields Eye Hospital. Neighbours hadn't really got to know them, but considered them a polite law-abiding couple. The shops and flats in Mayes Road were a solidly-built Victorian development and little domestic noise penetrated those solid walls, although the manager of the outfitters downstairs testified that there seemed to have been an unusual amount of movement on the stairs in the closing days of the year.

He had been so busy with the annual sale that he couldn't be any more precise. On the night of 31st December 1999, most locals were out celebrating, either in Trafalgar Square or in one of the many North London pubs, and three or four revellers returning at about two or three o'clock thought they heard sounds of an angry quarrel coming from one of the flats over the shops – although their state of inebriation made them rather unreliable witnesses.

The nurse failed to turn up for her shift at 8am on Monday 3rd January, and there was no answer when the ward clerk rang her home telephone. Her husband's employers were not expecting him at work until the Wednesday. The absence of relatives in UK meant that when the police were eventually alerted, ten days of the new year had passed.

After forcing entry into the flat a grim scene met the officers. Although they had seen corpses before, none were so badly mutilated as that of Mrs. Janet Hendricks. It took a week to clean the apartment of bloodstains, according to the tabloids.

The obvious suspect was Pieter, Janet's husband, and a national manhunt was launched on 10th January, widened to include Interpol when it was discovered that he had caught a flight to Helsinki in the early hours of 2nd January. Despite intensive searches and numerous reported sightings from Prague to Kiev over six years, he had still not been traced. There was no shortage of theories of his death or re-emergence somewhere under an assumed identity. It was even suggested in some quarters that he was back in UK.

All the details of the murder, so vividly described in the tabloids, were being recalled by Sharon as the taxi came to a halt in the congestion at Manor House. Fantasies were starting to fill her mind, and she seriously contemplated opening the door and running, when traffic started to flow once more. At least he's taking me home she thought, relieved that he had not turned left into the evening gloom of Finsbury Park.

Sharon was by now quite unable to maintain the empty chatter with the cabbie as she sat willing the traffic to clear and the minutes to pass. She never thought she would be so relieved to see Wood Green High Road and to feel the taxi speeding along the bus lane and past the green light for the left turn into Mayes Road. The cabbie needed no guidance to no. 152, drew to a halt and turned to Sharon to confirm the meter reading. Upon seeing Sharon's face be let out an exclamation.

"Good God! Your face is white as a sheet! Oh, I'm so sorry, I've scared you, haven't I? The murder... and everything. The fact is, I've been as upset as you are, just wishing I could get this journey over with. I was one of the two policeman who broke into your flat." His voice trembled as he continued, "The force gave us both a week's trauma leave, but then there was the inquest... Fact is, I had a complete breakdown a month after being back at work. After a lot of sessions with counsellors and therapists, I was eventually able to face the world again, and a taxi-driver mate helped me get this job. But I still can't talk about that flat, and it nearly put me back with the shrinks when you said your address..."

* * *

Going for Gold   *Mary Richard*

The sound of raised angry voices stirred Joseph from his day-dreaming. Looking up, he realised his horse and cart had come to a halt and that the horse was steadily munching apples from one of the trees lining the edge of the orchard. Shaking the reins he hastened the horse on its way, doffing his cap and apologising profusely. Yet again his day-dreaming had got him into trouble; but it wasn't just day-dreaming.

He was tired of delivering bread for the family bakery and he didn't want to be an apprentice baker like his younger brother. He wanted adventure and to see more of the world. Joseph, (Joe to his family and friends), and his friend Silas would often sit in their local inn planning and scheming how to escape their daily humdrum lives in the remote rural Warwickshire village and make their way up in the world.

They would look on with envy at the lives of the landed gentry and the upper classes. In Victorian England position and status was everything. Classism created the systemic oppression of lower and middle classes to the advantage of those upper classes.

Silas was a discontented chap, a cup half-empty kind of person for whom other people's fortune was his misfortune. He looked up to Joe who was a larger-than-life character, not just in personality but also in build and with an impressive black bushy beard. Joe was popular at the local inn and could spin a good yarn; Silas and his family worked the land and lived in a small tied cottage. The hours were long and the pay poor.

Joe and Silas would sometimes risk a little poaching to supplement their incomes. Both were united in their dreams of adventure and making their fortune, so decided to save as much as they could; even if it meant a little more poaching and a little less beer!

Joe arranged with the local dairy to include milk deliveries on his bread round and Silas found extra work as a chimney sweep which he fitted in on his one day off a week.

Months passed, until one evening, whilst supping a pint, Joe picked up a newspaper left on the bench beside him. Joe leapt up waving the paper and shouting excitedly.

"This is it; this is the answer!" Silas, unable to read, caught Joe's excitement and asked him to read it out. It was the summer of 1848 and the headlines declared 'Californian Gold'. The pair read on with mounting excitement – could this be the answer to their dreams, not just for adventure but making their fortunes as well? With naïve confidence they made their plans.

Six months later, having sailed on a clipper from Liverpool to America and undertaking a trek of several thousand miles through rough terrain they arrived at Sutter's Mill, California. The journey overland had been made by wagon-train with hundreds of other hopefuls and would-be prospectors. Conditions were treacherous and food and water in short supply. Many succumbed to cholera; the deadly disease became a far greater threat than the native Americans, who were angry at their land being taken from them. Having survived the journey, Joe and Silas were billeted in a tent at one of the camps around the area known as Poverty Bar.

Prospecting was extremely hard work and for little return. Though thousands of men and women joined the rush, few struck it rich and many soon returned home defeated and disappointed. The living conditions were primitive, and danger lurked amongst the hard-bitten, lawless, and often violent men struggling to survive and desperate to find gold at any price.

Joe and Silas moved from camp to camp in their search for gold. They had, over many weeks, managed to accumulate a small amount between them. Joe also managed to make a little money utilising his knowledge and skills of baking by making bread for the other prospectors, but the money earnt from this was minimal. They too were considering returning home, disappointed with the amount of gold they had accrued and somewhat disillusioned by the experience. Between them the gold was not going to bring the kind of riches and freedoms they both desired.

One night, whilst Joe was sleeping, some sixth sense brought him instantly awake. With a start, he saw Silas kneeling astride him with a wild look in his eye and a large claw-hammer raised high above his head. ready to strike. In one swift movement, Joe brought his knees up and twisted at the hip, throwing the smaller, lighter Silas off-balance and onto the ground beside him. In a flash, Joe was sitting astride Silas and had wrenched the hammer from his grasp. Silas was struggling to escape Joe's grip.

The commotion woke the other occupants of the tent. Realising what had happened, they went to Joe's aid. Recognising the enormity of what he had tried to do and the futility of his situation, Silas stopped struggling and lay there subdued and silently crying.

Joe could see that the conditions under which they had been living and working for the last few months and the disappointing outcome, had caused Silas to crack. They agreed to share what little gold they had and go their separate ways.

Joe decided to return to England alone and never saw or heard from Silas again. He visited Silas' parents but did not reveal the true story behind his lone return. Months later he heard that Silas had returned to England and was working at the dockyards in Liverpool.

Joe put his gold towards the purchase of a small holding of about 30 acres. Within five years, he had married and had a family of four, but he still craved adventure and still enjoyed a pint or two. His wife would sometimes say that the only reason Joe arrived home safely from the inn was because the horse knew the way home and Joe would often be found flat on his back on the floor of the cart, snoring loudly!

There were times when Joe, being restless, would, without recourse, load the horse and cart and disappear for several weeks at a time.

In 1858 when news broke of gold being found in Denver, Colorado, Joe did not hesitate. This time, he managed to persuade his brother Henry to join him. Joe reckoned that his brother could provide bread for the prospectors whilst he panned for gold. He left his long-suffering and tolerant wife to look after the small holding with her parents and undertook the long journey to Denver.

Joe and his brother staked a claim on a plot beside the South Platte River near Idaho Springs. Here, they did strike gold. However, during the rush, numerous eighty-foot pines had been uprooted to enable camps to be set up. This had impacted on the environment and the native people working the land. To compensate, the government insisted, as condition of a claim, that prospectors had to plant trees and pay taxes. Unfortunately, Joe and his brother failed to meet either condition and their land was forfeited but not before they managed to accumulate a fair amount of gold.

They returned to England triumphant, but after months of travelling they were tired and weary and wrapped up in their thoughts of home and reuniting with their families. They were on the last leg of their journey at Euston station. Whilst waiting for the train north, they stowed their carpet bag of gold under the bench on which they were seated...

They boarded the train each thinking the other had retrieved the precious cargo. Not so! As the train pulled away from the station the awful realisation dawned. All they could do was wait until they reached the next station, then make the return journey.

Never had a journey seemed so slow. They ran to the platform and to their utter amazement the bag remained where they had left it. They hugged each other with glee and waited for the next train, with the bag held firmly between them.

Their return home was a joyous event. The gold they had worked so hard for enabled Henry to set up his own bakery, whilst Joe and his family purchased extra land which turned their small holding into a farm of one hundred and thirty acres.

Life was settled for a while, and Joe kept the locals amused with tales of his travels. Then came news of mining opportunities in Russia for gold and diamonds... but that's a story for another time!

* * *

10 Words

Writer's Block

By Gordon Reece Davies

Writer's block...

Sudden inspiration!

Story told in just ten words

***

Velsheda   *David Gee*

A lifetime memory.

Sailing has always been my passion so you can imagine my excitement when I received an invitation to crew Velsheda for the Round the Island Race. This is a handicapped 60-mile circuit of the Isle of Wight and a world-famous annual event at what is considered the birthplace of world yachting.

The race starts and finishes at the Royal Yacht Squadron at Cowes. It takes place at the end of Cowes week in August, immediately before the Fastnet race. The event usually involves as many as 1600 assorted sailing craft.

At the start of the race, when all the boats line up, it is almost possible to cross from the Isle of Wight to the mainland jumping from deck to deck. The sight is unbelievable, and everyone is fully occupied attempting to avoid collisions, which are very frequent occurrences.

Velsheda is a magnificent and majestic classic 'J' class yacht, now some 88 years old. She and her two remaining cohorts Endeavour and Shamrock must hold a record for longevity. They are still racing and competing today. All have had a chequered career having been rescued by very wealthy individuals. They have all undergone numerous multi-million pound refits and restoration.

Velsheda is the only one of the remaining three still based in the UK. These beautiful, classical, yachts were built in the early 1930's purely for offshore racing. They all have majestic dimensions and stature.

Velsheda is some 39.4 m long (129 ft 3 inches). She has a beam 6.56 m (21 ft 6 inches), a displacement of some 143 tons and draws 4.57 m (15 ft) of water under her fin keel. She was built in steel in the world-famous

Camper and Nicholson yard at Gosport Hampshire to order by Mr. W.L. Stephenson, the owner and Managing Director of Woolworths, and completed in 1933. The cost at today's value would have been some 20 million pounds. She was named after Mr. Stephenson's three daughters Velma, Sheila, and Daphne. Velsheda is now Bermudan rigged and she has the tallest single steel mast afloat, some 175 ft and carries up to 10,000 sq. ft of sail, the equivalent area of 4 full sized tennis courts. The cost of operating her in the 1930's was awesome with a regular transit crew of 16 and a racing crew of 30. Between 1933, when she was commissioned, and 1939, Velsheda won over 40 international races.

Some ten 'J' class yachts were built in the early 1930's, literally regardless of expense, by multi-millionaires with the sole purpose to compete in international yacht racing. Regrettably only 3 of the original 10 'J' class yachts remain, all having been rescued from muddy creeks where they had been left to rot since the late 1930's.

Today, 'J' class racing has undergone a revival. Technologically further-advanced, and much faster, modern competition yachts have been built, but the world will never again see the grace of these early original ladies.

* * *

The Round the Island race is open to virtually anyone who has the skill and is equipped to meet competence and safety standards set by the scrutineers from the R.Y.A. For hundreds of people, including spectators, the Round the Island race is the highlight of the yacht sailing year. With multinational sponsorship, parties and celebrations are going on the whole week. Every mooring and marina is bursting to capacity, with yachts moored five deep from the quayside, marinas and pontoons.

Our party met at the coffee marquee, but we rapidly moved to the beer tent immediately it opened. Velsheda had been chartered by our hosts, a national bank. The charter came with a captain and three professional crew. The captain was a larger-than-life South African gentleman called Beau who did not take prisoners. There were eleven other invitees who were experienced amateur sailors. Beau wasted no time in telling us that we would have our work cut out trying to handle Velsheda in the congested waters with so few people as they normally raced with 25 crew. We would have no time to relax, and anyone looking for an easy two days, could leave now. He explained that Velsheda was moored on a commercial shipping buoy half a mile offshore because she was too big to be accommodated in the Marina and, by the way, she did not have an engine. He explained that the rest of the day would be spent on a shakedown familiarisation cruise up and down the Solent for us to literally learn the ropes and break us in. We would then return to the buoy, be taken ashore that night by tender for dinner but would sleep on board, in order to be ready for the race the next morning.

He warned us this was serious stuff and because of the immense size and weight of the sails there was no room for carelessness or indecision. It was going to be physically extremely hard work. We then grabbed our kit-bags and climbed aboard a waiting motor launch which threaded its way through the packed Marina towards the moorings in Cowes Roads.

As we left the shelter of the river in the sunshine it was noticeable that the wind had increased to force 3/4 from the south-west, waves were beginning to increase in size and small white crests were beginning to form.

Velsheda was immediately visible. She stood out from the other moored vessels with her amazingly beautiful lines, snow white hull, and enormous 178 ft mast dwarfing all around her. As we got nearer, we could see her extensive open teak decks broken only by exceptionally large stainless-steel winches strategically placed around the deck. Replacement cost for any one of them would have been around the price of a new small car. All the blocks, running gear and cleats were on a similarly massive scale. There was no sheet or rope less than an inch in diameter and all were new and of the finest quality.

The mainsail boom was even more massive. It was about the thickness of four railway sleepers and at least 60 ft in length. It must have weighed well over a ton and the thought of controlling that in a strong wind as the ship went about was a terrifying thought. There was a small deckhouse towards the stern accommodating a companionway down to the interior below deck.

Behind the deckhouse was a very large helmsman's wheel with a curved stand to enable the helmsman to stand upright behind the wheel when the ship was heeling a 45 degree angle. I noticed there were no handrails or guard rails around the ship, the reason for this was obviously to prevent ropes or sails fouling them. The only thing to protect crew from falling overboard were stainless steel lifelines along the length of the deck where crew could attach their harnesses. There was also a steel toe rail where a crew member who slid down the deck could find some purchase until they could get a hand hold to pull themselves back up the deck. This toe rail would be submerged when the ship was heeling.

This old lady was no cruiser, and that anyone crewing her during a serious race had to be not only super strong but also show incredible competence, knowledge and durability. I also concluded that Beau was in no way exaggerating with his initial address to us.

After lunch we were broken into teams of three and given an area of responsibility. We also learned the duties of the two teams either side of us so that in an emergency we could interchange and support each other. My job, with two others, of solid stature was as a winch-ape.

I was stationed amidships with two of the monster winches and given the task of winding-in and trimming the jib sheets. One of us to tail the thick rope, another to actually wind the winch, and the third to release the jib as we went about. We needed to interchange as the winching had to be superfast and timed to the second.

The jib sheet was so vast that if we were late winching-in and it filled with wind, we would be trying to winch against anything from two to seven tons depending on the wind strength. Similarly, if the sheet had to be hardened-up, despite the size of the winches, it was heavy manual work with water coming over us and the boat often at an angle of 45 degrees.

Our set of winches also had the task of raising the mainsails from the boom up to the full 178 ft of the mast. We were, with others, also responsible for getting it down very quickly before the wind caught the 3/4 tons of sail, furling it around the massive boom and placing the sail cover on.

That first afternoon we sailed down the Solent to the Needles and back. The wind stiffened and we were thrilled at the power and speed as the old girl picked up her skirts and ran. In the short sharp sea with a force 5 wind on her beam and heeling at some 45 degrees we hit nearly 13 knots and we were soaked with spray and bone weary. We returned to the buoy off Cowes and after a shower and change of clothes the tender took us into Cowes where our hosts entertained us to a superb dinner. The wine had flowed very liberally. Most of us were barely conscious. Getting back on board from the tender to Velsheda at 2:00 a.m. in the pitch dark with a sea running was a spectacle to behold as was finding our respective bunks!

The next morning was Race Day. We hit the coffee, Anadin and Paracetamol big time. We had to dig deep into our will power to get going. During the night it had rained, and the wind was force 4 blustering 5 with white horses. This was in the Solent which is relatively sheltered, so going around the western end of the Isle of Wight we were expecting some rough water.

* * *

The start of the race was incredible. The sea state was quite rough with wind over quite a strong running tide. Some 1600 boats were spread across the Solent, from Cowes to the mainland, all milling about, several colliding in the melee, trying to keep behind the start line. Many failed and had to go about, sail back and go about again to sail up to the start line. It was chaotic. Most boats gave us a reasonably wide berth as our size and bulk and steel hull would have done them no good at all had they collided with us

With our sail area we did not need to be at the front as we knew we could power through the fleet. We therefore hung back, luffed-up into the wind and watched the entertainment taking place all around us. We marked the start time with a stopwatch in case we did not hear the start cannon. As it was, we did and saw the puff of smoke. We came about, hardened the sheets and soon reached 13 knots, heeling right over with spray and water flying everywhere.

We had to be super careful as we were soon powering through the fleet and boats were literally everywhere around us, some very close indeed. 150 tons of steel travelling at 13 knots can do a lot of damage.

We were doing very well for about an hour until tragedy struck. We had a very strong gust of wind and a noise like a cannon shot came from the mast head. The mainsail had split from mid-mast and was flapping about uselessly. We immediately lost way and had to spend the next hour and a half fighting several-hundred square yards of wet sail in strong winds and rigging a jury rig.

We did complete the race at half speed and arrived at the finish line many hours later. Of course, we did not win, but our memories were indelible. We all learned a tremendous amount about true sailing and I for one will never forget my Velsheda experience.

* * *

The Key Witness   *Norma Hall*

It was still dark when Tawanda woke up in his small hard bed, his bare arms hastily pulling up the thin sheet against the cold and his stomach rumbling. He could hear a stray dog barking in the distance and then gradually the calls of the women as they set off to fetch water from the well, as the first light of the new day crept over the horizon.

Tawanda knew he mustn't delay as it was a long way to school and he needed to get there early as today was going to be special. Jumping up, he tried not to disturb his sleeping brother and sister, pulling aside the old curtain that separated their part of the family hut and slipping past his still-snoring father. He wiped the sleep from his eyes as he found his mauve blazer, the one he'd been so happy to finally get and put on his khaki shorts and shirt. His tackies completed the outfit, still a bit big as they'd been his traditional Xmas present to replace the old worn ones he'd had before

"Plenty of room to grow into," Amai, his mother had told him proudly.

Then it was off, his school bag trailing behind him as he ran, black crows scattering and cawing, flying up into the msasa trees as he passed.

It was a long way through the bush and dried-up river beds but Tawanda knew the best paths to take and didn't stop running until he could see his school finally coming into view. Other boys and girls were also arriving as he came up to the whitewashed building, an imposing structure built by the missionaries, with a few remaining Jesuits and nuns on the staff of now otherwise native Zimbabweans.

Tawanda peeped into the assembly hall and smiled as he saw it laid out for the great occasion which was to follow later that day. It was prize day and it already looked impressive with the desks and chairs in place on the small wooden stage and benches for parents in the main body of the hall. At the back were trestle tables where the tea and cakes would be served. Tawanda's mouth watered at the thought. It seemed a long time until he'd get his meagre ration of sadza after lessons at lunch time.

He watched as the white table-cloths went onto the table, cups and saucers clattered into place and then as the wooden doors were pushed aside for the man delivering boxes of cakes for the ensuing parents' celebration.

In a moment of madness, Tawanda saw the room had emptied for just a second and he ran forward and took one of the cream-filled doughnuts, raising it quickly to his mouth in a vain attempt to demolish the evidence.

Vain indeed, for although he'd thought he'd got away with it and happily went through his lessons that morning, just before breaktime his name was called to go and see the headmaster. Tawanda held his breath as he knocked and entered the Lion's den. Elijah 'Success' Gono, the largest prefect stood in front of Father O'Driscoll, his arms folded across his puffed-out chest.

"Now Elijah", said the Father, 'Tell us what you told me before.' Elijah's smirking account of what he'd seen Tawanda do followed and then, from the Head:

"Aha! So you see, Tawanda, we have a key witness here; a witness to your transgressions. This is a Christian school and we don't steal. You'll have to be taught a lesson, so don't expect to get your class prize this afternoon. I'm very disappointed in you."

The parents had arrived and were waiting in the Hall. The Guest of Honour, Didymus Nyemba, the local MP, was not renowned for his punctuality but the crowd was used to waiting for their dignitaries. Finally, a white Land-Cruiser with blacked-out windows came speeding up the dusty school drive and a large man in a smart blue suit stepped out accompanied by his two security guards. Taking off his sunglasses, he entered the school building and was ushered onto the stage by Father O'Driscoll.

The speeches and prize giving rambled on with the familiar ululation of all the excited parents – all except Tawanda's of course, as his puzzled Amai looked over her shoulder to the back of the hall to see what had happened to her errant son. She couldn't understand it as he'd seemed so proud when he'd told them of his forthcoming class prize for achievement.

At last, it was time for the tea and cakes; second only to the top prizes in excitement, and as usual the plates of delicious cakes were rapidly demolished. Not only quickly eaten up but bundled furtively into open handbags or coat pockets. The parents saw nothing like the lavish culinary display before them, except on this one day of the school calendar and were certainly not going to miss their one chance to stock up. Elijah 'Success' Gono was among them stuffing his mouth, his puffed-out chest seemingly growing wider as he munched.

The guest of Honour had rushed off to an important meeting at a 5-star Hotel in the nearest regional centre, so had declined to stay. Some said they'd glimpsed a glamorous woman waiting in the Land-Cruiser when the door was opened for his departure.

Tawanda back in his bare classroom, sat hunched over his desk. He thought of his old library book story by Charles Dickens and felt like a poor Oliver Twist who'd been punished for only wanting a little more. He wished he could rather be in a Harry Potter book and cast a spell, or rise above the crowd on his broom stick. He'd certainly like to have waved away that Elijah, the key witness.

Baba, his father, when told about it all later, had no qualms.

"Well, Tawanda, it's just life you see. Those chefs and others in authority always take the most and get richer while the poor like us, don't even get to feed on the crumbs."

Amai wasn't as understanding and gave Tawanda a clip around the ear for spoiling this one chance she'd had of showing off her clever son.

* * *

Flying on the Extreme Right Wing

Richard Hughes

The Ministers and Bishops are in cahoots (again)
Now the world is flat again.
Science is magic again.
Magic, heresy;
Heresy, sin.
Sin is everywhere.
All of us have it.
It cannot be borne.
Bear it, however, we must.

Kowtow
Respect.
Lobotomize you babies in prayer.
Heads down,
Eyes forward.
Study astrology, numerology,
Eugenics.
Please turn out the lights when you're done.
Oh!
There are no lights.

* * *

Images of Scilly   *Hazel Lintott*

Seagulls calling, wailing, screeching, perched upon the highest ledges

Into night and early morning, squabbling, jostling, calling, calling.

Around Mincarlo's granite rocks little puffins gently bobbing

Adding jazzy stripes of colour to the ancient rockface rising.

Soft St Martin's duney beaches stretch into the opal sea.

Hear the oyster catcher piping, lonely call on breezes whispering.

Tresco Abbey's sheltered garden hears exotic peacocks calling.

Flowers and palms luxuriant tumbling; see red squirrels shy and trembling.

Bold St Mary's harbour's waiting for the boat which once a day

Brings the lifeblood of the islands whether seas are stormy, racing,

Whether skies are blue or grey.

In the shallow waters joining Tresco, Bryher, Samson too,

You can see the sand reflecting through the water's turquoise blue.

You can trace the ancient field walls of a landscape that was thriving,

Now submerged beneath the water, covered with the sand that's shifting

Drifting to the water's call.

In the distance sits 'The Bishop' keeping guard for ships at sea.

Through the darkest night its flashing warns that Scilly's rocks are waiting

For another tragedy.

The jagged Western Rocks protect the islands from the wild, breaking

Waves and storms that, unrelenting, sweep across the open sea.

And all around the gulls are wheeling, perched upon the highest ledges.

Into night and early morning, squabbling, jostling, calling, calling...

* * *

10 Words

The Fairground
By Mary Richard

He held his breath in anticipation... as the claws hovered.

***

A Photo Falls to the Floor
Mike Gardiner

Angela Merridew looked from the window of her second-floor flat and felt sorry for those going into the food bank in the church hall opposite. But only a little sorry, for why weren't these people better organised? Why did they run out of food? Angela had lived by herself for some forty years and had, you might say, perfected the art of self-sufficiency.

Her parents had left her enough money to buy a one-bedroomed flat in an unfashionable North London suburb, which had been convenient enough for commuting to her job as a typist in a city office, though in her retirement it was a rather dreary environment. But let no one say that Angela was unhappy. Angela was content. Her life was as self-contained as a box of Dairy Milk chocolates; though from time to time, Angela allowed herself a moment of self-pity, reflecting on her disappointment that no man had ever picked a choice confection from the box. In these days of exciting gift-wrapped Thornton's Belgian delights, perhaps Cadbury's Dairy Milk was not as appealing as it had once seemed. But Angela was content.

Ever since the onset of arthritis in her shoulder, she had had her small weekly grocery order delivered by Sainsbury's. It rarely changed, because she saw no reason to change it. She enjoyed starting the day with Alpen fruit-and-nut muesli, followed by one thin, lightly-toasted slice of wholemeal bread, spread with Frank Cooper's Fine Cut marmalade. Lunch was a low-fat yoghourt with a carefully prepared fruit salad. Then, on a fine day, Angela might walk to the local park and after gently walking the perimeter, take a seat and pass the time quietly watching people.

Sometimes someone would smile and say good afternoon to the neatly-dressed lady on the park bench and Angela would cautiously return the smile and the greeting. She did not encourage any communication beyond this; for after all, if a friendship developed, heaven alone knew what disruption to her routine that might lead to. In cold weather, Angela liked to catch a bus to a bustling High Street a couple of miles away, and amuse herself browsing through the department stores and fashion outlets; for she took great pride in her appearance, even on days when she didn't meet another soul.

Returning from her afternoon outing, Angela would carefully lay the table for her dinner at 6 o'clock. Here, Angela allowed herself some variation. Sometimes it was a cottage pie she had cooked, with the other half carefully packaged, dated and stored in the freezer; at other times, perhaps an omelette or chicken casserole, always home-cooked. Rarely would she order a ready-prepared dish from the supermarket, and certainly never anything foreign like curry or pasta.

After a leisurely evening meal, she would clear the table, put on her gloves and wash the dishes, then play back the BBC early evening news, which was recorded at 6 o'clock. What was left of the evening often included a TV programme that interested her, especially one of those increasingly popular travel series, for Angela liked to travel the world through her TV screen. After soaking in her bath, she would relax in bed with a chapter or two of Jane Austen or Mary Stewart whilst sipping a glass of sherry, until her bedside lamp was switched off, always by half past ten.

Angela was contented. At peace whilst nothing disturbed her routine. She would say that she had a very fulfilling life. One or two office colleagues had suggested keeping in touch after retirement, but Angela had sent only brief replies to their emails and phone calls, and had shown no enthusiasm for a reunion. If one were to ask who her friends were, she would probably mention her elder sister, married many years but with no children.

Barbara lived in Plymouth and she and her husband seemed to have such busy lives, what with their music, their bridge, and their activities with a group called 'u3a.' Barbara and Edward had visited Angela's small flat once, but the day had been such a disaster that it had not been worth repeating. Instead, Barbara would ring her sister every Sunday and tell her what interesting things she and her husband had been doing during the week.

It was rare for Angela to receive a handwritten letter. But this morning, among the special offers and reminders of insurances falling due there was a white envelope addressed in a firm upright hand to Miss A. Merridew. The name of the apartment block was spelt wrongly and the post code had incorrect digits, but with their usual ingenuity the post office had delivered it to the right address. Angela frowned and studied the postmark, somewhere in a northern county, and the handwriting, which did not belong to any of the small circle of people who might write to her. And they would all have known her precise address. She carefully slit open the envelope with her ivory-handled letter-opener, and a photo fell out and landed face down on the floor. On the back was written in fading pencil 'August 1976.'

Angela needed only a moment's thought for long-buried painful memories to come flooding back. It had been a wonderful holiday in Jersey, when the sun shone all day and carefree days were spent in the company of Eric, a lovely man a couple of years older than her. They were both quiet, thoughtful people, and each had tentatively tried this holiday for 18-25s. They had found they shared a love of books and country walks, and the seven days walking and talking had passed so quickly. After the holiday, Angela had written a couple of times to Eric, but he had never replied.

Angela unfolded the single sheet of notepaper with the printed heading 'Janet and Eric Day' and read,

'Dear Anthea,

Janet and I were turning out some boxes of old photos and came upon this lovely picture of us on the beach in Jersey. Do you remember? My wife wanted to throw it away, but I thought you might like it, provided you are still at the same address, though I guess you must be somewhere far away happily married with children and grandchildren, Yours sincerely, Eric Day'.

Angela didn't want to look at the photo. She carefully picked it up and carried it to the pedal bin and deposited it there with the letter. She sat down at the breakfast table and put a slice of wholemeal in the toaster.

A tear ran down her cheek. He had called her Anthea.

* * *

Photoshock   *Gordon Reece Davies*

Norton Harper stepped off the escalator and hastened towards the west-bound platform. Already the atmosphere in the tube station was uncomfortably hot and the air felt thick with the oppressively stale smell of underground systems the world over. A young woman wearing headphones jostled past him. The man in front of him halted suddenly and turned around. Unable to stop in time Norton walked straight into him.

"Sorry, mate, wrong platform!"

The man fought his way back down the narrow passageway against the oncoming torrent of commuters. In the confusion of the incident Norton lost his grip on his instrument-case and it dropped to the floor. He stooped to retrieve it. Immediately a briefcase caught him on the ear and he was swung off balance and went down on one knee. Someone kicked the violin case and his precious instrument went skittering down the passage towards the platform. As Norton reached for it another commuter stumbled over his arm. The man regained his balance, turning back to hold out a steadying arm and help Norton back to his feet.

"I'm so sorry, are you alright?" he took Norton's arm and guided him to one side "Just take a moment here to get your breath back."

"But my instrument..." Norton looked around. A middle-aged lady had picked it up and was walking back towards them. "Thank you, thank you," he grabbed the leather case and dusted it off. Like a prize-fighter's skin, a patina of scars and bruises marked every step of its career and now it had another scuff-mark to commemorate today's rehearsal. Norton turned to thank his rescuers, but they were gone. He made his way gratefully toward the platform. He'd leave checking his instrument for damage until he got to the Albert Hall, you didn't risk showing off a valuable violin on a tube train.

He checked the time, eight forty, with luck he'd still make it before nine. Sir Jeffrey didn't take kindly to late arrivals. But for God's sake, what an absurd time for rehearsals; central London in the rush-hour was no joke. There was another rehearsal scheduled tomorrow and a full run-through on Thursday, both for the same time, before Friday evening's concert (at least that would be a more civilised time). Norton tried to calm his thoughts down. He began looking around the carriage at his fellow passengers.

Within a couple of minutes, he found himself playing 'Sherlock.' The idea was to look carefully at the travelers and try to deduce something about them from their appearance. As a young teenager he'd played it with his brother whenever they travelled by tube and it had caused a lot of hilarity and good-natured fun between them. Now, it was a little guilty pleasure he sometimes allowed himself.

The man standing near the doors, broad chested with a paunch like a cello, his weather-beaten bald-head burned chestnut brown by the sun – he was a gardener for sure. The give-away was the liberal amount of mud on his work boots and the legs of his jeans. He awarded himself five points, it had been far too easy. He turned his attention to the young woman sitting opposite.

Smartly dressed in a black trouser suit with a white blouse under a wide-brimmed black hat in some sort of a straw finish. She wore glasses with a heavy graphite-grey frame and a sturdy pair of shoes. Norton decided she must be some sort of lawyer – a solicitor or barrister perhaps.

That was until he noticed the case at her feet. Larger, but slimmer than a briefcase, it was made from aluminium with riveted corner reinforcements and a robust carry-handle. Not the sort of case for legal papers, too slim to carry a barrister's wig and unsuitable for photographic equipment. He was familiar with the cases for most musical instruments and it looked nothing like anything he'd ever seen before. Norton was puzzled. He looked at her face, quite an attractive face, carefully made-up, he could see that behind her dark-rimmed spectacles, her eyes were constantly moving as though watching out for someone or something.

He hadn't realised he was staring at her quite so blatantly until her eyes fixed on his in a clear challenge. She gave the merest hint of a smile as he turned away. Norton was intrigued, she wasn't a lawyer then, or a photographer and unlikely to be a musician. She was clearly self-assured but at the same time constantly vigilant.

The key to her identity clearly was tied-in to the contents of that strange-looking case. He thought about it carefully and was beginning to come up with an outlandish idea which would have won him a heap of points when playing the game with his brother.

Norton got up to leave the train at South Kensington and noticed that the young woman alighted at the same stop. She moved ahead of him and soon disappeared into the crowd.

* * *

The rehearsal had been tedious to say the least. Sir Jefferey had lived up to his reputation for being pernickety. He'd had the woodwind section play the same passage through at least twenty times while the rest of the orchestra twiddled their thumbs. Then he'd turned his attentions to the strings and given them the benefit of his famously bad temper. Norton was pleased to be heading home.

As he took his seat on the Brighton-Line train at Victoria Station, the young woman with the strange looking case sat down beside him.

"So, we meet again – I was sitting opposite you this morning."

"Er, Yes, that's right – Look, I'm sorry if I appeared to be staring at you, I didn't intend to cause embarrassment." Norton could feel his cheeks burning.

"Think nothing of it, I was watching you – you were playing the Face Game, weren't you?"

"The Face Game?"

"Yes, trying to guess someone's occupation from what they look like. I've got you down as a concert violinist, am I right?"

"More-or-less," said Norton, "I used to play that game with my brother when we were small, we called it Sherlock."

"So how many points do I get for being more-or-less right? And what did you have me down as?"

"Five points, an extra five if it's a wacky idea and bonus twenty if it's proven true. You'll laugh, I couldn't work out what you've got in that case so I settled for the wacky five points. I guessed it's probably one of those collapsible sniper-rifles you see in the spy movies, so I reckon you're either a secret agent or a hit-man."

She laughed "Wow, you're too good at this game, five well deserved points, hit-man it is! But I prefer to call it waste-disposal."

Norton thought things were going rather well. A bit of harmless flirtation with this rather attractive young lady and who knows what might become of it?

"So how does it work? This hit-man business, is it profitable?"

"Very", she said. "I get a photo of the target, follow him or her for a day or two and then I take them down when they least expect it."

"And do you always use the sniper-rifle?" Norton was enjoying this little fantasy.

"No, there are twenty-seven different ways to bump someone off, I do whatever is appropriate." She looked him in the eye and smiled her enigmatic smile.

"My stop coming up, I'll see you around."

She walked towards the doors and reached into the pocket of her suit for her rail ticket. As she withdrew her hand, a photograph fluttered onto the floor, landing face-down. The automatic doors opened and she stepped out.

Norton ran to pick up the dropped photo and stepped onto the platform to give it back to her. She was nowhere to be seen. He heard the train doors slide closed and it rattled away.

Norton turned the photograph over and stared at it in disbelief. The face staring back at him from the photograph was his own and a line had been drawn diagonally across it in felt-tip pen.

A hand reached from behind to hold his shoulder firmly and a familiar voice said:

"Congratulations you get the twenty bonus points!" He felt a pressure against his back but he barely felt the blade as it slipped between his ribs to penetrate his heart...

* * *

10 Words

A Short Story
by Mike Gardiner

Revenge murder of Agatha lands Belgian in little grey cell.

* * *

Not What They Expected
Norma Hall

Even when they first arrived, it was not what they expected. The couple were looking forward to seeing Tiverton as a possible place to move to and perhaps that had given them unrealistic expectations. Instead of the lovely river they'd hoped for, they had driven over a semi-polluted stretch of dark water, concrete sides to the bridge, before turning into a road of free – almost deserted – parking. Leaving the car beside an old church, they entered the overgrown grounds and walked around the grey unwelcoming building, peering over the hedge, to catch a glimpse of the elusive river.

Sunlight shone wanly as they left the churchyard and made their way past boarded-up ruins of an old castle, towards a sign indicating the marketplace. A stream of teenage children, coming up the hill in twos and threes after school, pushed past the couple on the narrow pavement. They had disappeared by the time the pair rounded the corner and found the deserted market building.

And the pattern continued. Looking for the high street, the couple passed rows of closed shops and premises. It was surely the main thoroughfare but looked uninviting with its betting shops, Iceland and seedy looking take-aways. Only one barbershop seemed to be open, where a few boys could be seen through the window having their hair cut. They passed a notice over a small alleyway indicating guitar lessons and a mother, with a small child clutching a guitar, passed them heading towards it. Otherwise, all was quiet.

The couple sat on an empty bench next to a clock tower where the time never moved. A small stream over the road headed out of the town and they watched a mother duck with thirteen new ducklings swimming. There were no further signs of life.

"Well, I'm certainly not going to live here," Morag exclaimed. Tim silently agreed but it took forty minutes to find their way back to the car – the empty streets merging into one another, trying to retrace the way they had come.

With time on their hands, the couple decided to go to Exmoor, before checking into the accommodation booked for the night. Being on the edge of Exmoor, they could get there quite easily after seeing some sights. Driving out of town, they passed empty looking supermarkets, and a leisure centre, but few other cars on the road.

"Doesn't anyone live down here then?", Morag queried, grumpily adding, "Well, I'm not that surprised, who'd want to!" Tim put it down to her disappointment at not liking the place, but he couldn't really disagree.

The weather changed as they drove towards the moors. Morag wondered if it was Arthur Conan Doyle country, it looked intimidating with windswept trees crouching over the pale gorse, remarking that she almost expected a black hound to stalk across the road.

"That's Dartmoor," Tim corrected, reminding her it was Lorna Doone country that they should expect, this being Exmoor.

They wound their way up the road to Haddon Hill, the nearest viewpoint, parking near the top and clambered up to see the view. Wimblehall Lake was in the distance and further off, the sandstone Dunkery Beacon, with the sea beyond. The view was spectacular. Morag, letting out her breath, had to admit it was well worth the visit and didn't disappoint. No-one else was there, however, and they never saw another car on their descent.

It was a long drive towards Twichen, with endless narrow roads winding up and down. With only one lane, there were few areas to allow for passing, but they were the only car on the road. That was until coming out onto a slightly wider strip, a huge looking tractor appeared out of nowhere, the careless driver atop, nearly knocking them off the road.

Identifying the fir tree they had been told to look for, the couple turned and began driving down to the farmhouse. Morag spotted what she thought was a person or a scarecrow crouching under a nearby tree. It turned out to be a statue in ceramics, of a strange man reading a book, when Tim took a photo of it later.

There were several buildings clustered together in a hamlet and making sure they got the right entrance to drive down, they followed instructions to park behind the self-contained accommodation they had booked. Making their way along the wooden fence, they found the door with its keylock and inserted the code they'd been given.

No-one appeared to greet them, but everything seemed in good order, and they were pleasantly surprised with the apartment with its lounge, kitchen, double bedroom and the quality of the accommodation overall.

"Just as well," muttered Morag, "as no one would come out all this way otherwise." Tim didn't remind her that they'd mainly booked it because of its inexpensive price. The flat faced the wall at the back, but there was a small garden which they could sit out in – if it hadn't been quite so chilly.

The night passed peacefully, and they enjoyed the takeaway they'd earlier bought on their way down.

"Just as well," Morag reminded Tim, "as we wouldn't have been able to get anything in Tiverton."

Although there were numerous cars and farm vehicles parked outside the houses on the site, they only caught a glimpse of one woman walking a dog near the road. No one else was visible.

After a reasonable night's sleep and some breakfast, they set off to explore. Morag found a map of the area among the ancient pamphlets in the hallway, indicating a path in the nearby woodland accessible for walking. Looking it up, Tim had found the name of the settlement they were in. Blackmarston had a long history, including a great fire in 1877 at Blackmarston House and the village had been a thriving community for those with Learning Disabilities, before being disbanded under the 2010 Community Care Act.

"That explains the number of houses and settlements around us," Tim went on, "although I'm sure they're all bought and are privately owned now."

Retracing Tim's steps of the night before, they found the statue and woodland path nearby. A patch of forest brought them out into an area of heather moorland before more woods, and finally up rocks surrounding a steep waterfall. From there a deep valley descended and within it they could see farm buildings, sheds, and the first sign of people working on the land. As they descended, the workers stopped, some leaning on their rakes, or standing by their wheelbarrows, watching them silently.

A large ruddy-faced man stepped out of the main building, doffing his hat in a sweeping gesture and addressed the pair.

"Greetings, we were expecting you. Welcome to our Training Centre. Come and see what can be achieved when people are allowed to thrive and not be institutionalised or moved back into cities." Morag and Tim had no option but to allow themselves to be led around the crops, animal pens and workshops where cars and a number of tractors were being worked on. Standing aside to enable them to see their work, Tim could see a number of the men had some sort of disability or learning difficulty. What worried him though was their silence, with little evidence of laughter or participation. It would later strike him that what they showed was at best acquiescence and at worst fear.

Carver, their Leader was called, would not hear of them leaving. He evaded questions as to why they were in the valley and where they all lived, leaving the impression it was somehow outlawed or under-cover. Morag had noticed the repainting of some vehicles and couldn't help remembering the huge tractor they'd seen the day before bearing down on them being hastily driven away. Could they really be stolen?

'They must stay for the May Day ceremony later, hadn't they seen that it was a pink moon?' When Tim remonstrated that they needed to go, a gun was produced and the amazed and frightened twosome found themselves walking with hands up, as Carver force-marched them towards the barn.

As the barn door swung open, Tim took his chance and swinging it hard against the gun it dropped to the floor, a swearing Carver grappling after it. They ran as fast as they could and had made quite some distance before hearing the gun shots that followed. The steep waterfall saved them, the older pursuer couldn't make it and one of his followers slipped and fell on the wet surface.

"I hadn't expected you back," the landlady said, appearing as the couple hastily packed their belongings to take out to their car. "It's happened to me before, people not returning, that's why I always ask they leave the key in the keylock. It must be the moors that cast a spell, or that old rascal calling himself Carver Doone."

It was not what they had expected but then it was Lorna Doone country.

* * *

Background Note

Lorna Doone tells the story of a young boy John Ridd, whose father was killed by Scottish outlaws – the Doones. Exiled to a remote part of Exmoor, the Doones rob travellers and local farms, as highway men and cattle rustlers. John enters the forbidden Doone valley by climbing up a steep and difficult waterfall and meets Lorna, kidnapped as an infant. Years later he rescues her and as they marry, she is shot through Oare church window by the wicked Carver Doone. After a struggle, Carver perishes in a bog, Lorna recovers and all is well. The book was written by Richard Blackmore in the 1800's, who went to school in Tiverton.

Yeard   *Richard Hughes*

Throw away scissors, throw away razors, soap dishes
And bookings at Barbers
Go desert islanding.
Build shelters, hunt mythical creatures, catch and
release them.
Invent new food stuffs.
Plant 1,000 acres and harvest a bumper crop.
Resist the urge to found a dynasty

Come home again
Push over Elephants in the square (metaphorically).
Beat your chest, celebrate
The hirsute fabulous you've become.
New for the New Age, skinny legged clear of thought
Looking like a 19th Century artisan.
Being a new Adam in a godless improved future.
Arthur Clarke's Star Child thinking
What next, what next?

* * *

The Salmon Leap   *Carol Merrett*

Morning water gurgling gently, gushing over paintbox
pebbles,
Our rainbow colours reflecting in the crystal depths.
Clear and pure, teasing ripples reaching to the
riverbank,
Encouraging each other to move, to play, to dance in
the tropical sunlight,
Listening to the music of the trees, of rustling leaves,
of babbling fish.
We were lazy, languorous, sensuously lapping against
reeds and weeds,
Encouraging the otters to join in our jollity, our fun
and games,
Laughing as birds dived into our glistening depths,
seeking the elusive minnows.
Such a joyous existence in the balmy warmth of
summer.

Darkening clouds as a rainstorm threatens above us,
Menacing our waters, we shiver tremulously,
As the heavens unleash their buckets chilling shards
of raindrops,
Bouncing dramatically, their pounding power sullying
our purity,
As we floundered, striving valiantly,
Churning our waters, throwing our power down into
the depths, defiant,
Unwilling to succumb to the mastery of the storm.

Staying strong, swirling, stirring, clinging to the rocks,
the grasses,
Until the storm, tired of the battle, breathed its last
gust of black-tipped needles,
Sighed and rushed away to torment another watery
victim.
We sighed, relaxed, too tired to play again, our waters
calmly subsiding.

Hark, listen... whispers from downstream reach our
ears.
Silent whispers become murmurs, quivering murmurs
become rumours,
Rumours become pulsating truth.
We thank the rain, the November storm has excited
our friends,
Awakened their senses,
Their natural intuition spurring them on.
We ripple excitedly, conscious of the excitement,
listening avidly,
Encouraging in our swelling movements,
waiting...waiting...waiting...
Another rumour reaches our banks from below.

/Over

"They're coming, they're coming…!"
Chattering excitedly, we splash, chuckling huge waves of glee into the rushing air,
Anticipating their arrival, voices rippling around the gleaming pebbles,
Against the verdant bank where otters peek out expectantly.
No longer a rumour, it is real, our excitement is electric,
Our power increases, throwing droplets into the air,
Eddies of crystal-clear water awaiting the moment.

Around the curve of the tumbling River Shin they slide into view.
Mounting, dancing, sun glinting from their sparkling, glistening scales,
A thunder of fins flapping, jumping, skipping the waves,
Leaping out of sheer joie de vivre,
Enjoying their flight, passionate and hungry to reach journey's end.
Waves lurch and lunge, cosseting, teasing, paddling around them.
We watch in awe, holding our watery breath in happiness.
Yes, it is true. The salmon have leapt into a fulfilling, fertile new life.

* * *

The Christmas Tree   *Polly Paice*

Getting ready for Christmas
I was looking for the tree
I rummaged in the cupboard,
Turned round and bumped my knee!

The tree finally erected
I was putting the angel on top
I wobbled and grabbed at the branches
And ended up under the lot!

I started again with that damned tree
Angel positioned on high
But then I tripped on the light lead
and fused all the blooming lights!

I groped my way to the fuse box
And tripped all the switches I guessed
Pleased with myself I returned
Not noticing the freezer chest.

When getting the food out later
I spotted the puddle on the floor
I slipped on the water, and staggered
Hitting my arm on the door!

Dinner over and feeling quite sore
I sat down and rested my knee
Then feeling slightly better
I tried once more with the tree.

This time I was really quite careful
Did everything perfectly right
I got down off the ladder
Then out went the perishing lights.

I tried all the bulbs in succession
I found one, and proceeded to mend
I must have touched a live wire
And my hair stood up on end.

Well, that's my story of Christmas
And that flipping Christmas tree
I must admit I really enjoyed
Spending Christmas in A&E!

* * *

The Shepherd's Carol   *Carol Merrett*

While angels soared silently above a frozen land on wings of gold

Shepherds quietly, wordlessly huddled uncomplainingly below

Watched over by an omnipotent God

Their eyes constantly twitching, blinking, lovingly seeking their wandering

Flocks, all munching contentedly, oblivious to the powerful presence quivering around them.

By daybreak, as the first threads of a golden dawn streaked across a sun-kissed sky, banishing the

Night, its fear, mystery and dark hidden depths crushed by the piercing light

All trembling fears were lifted, erased from the shepherds' anxious minds.

Seated stiffly, they sighed, smiled gently, rubbing their frozen fingers, stretched their night-weary limbs, lowering their blankets slowly

On to the grassy, frost-painted meadow and, in

The all-encompassing silence, which filled the awesome heavens and its obedient earth, they fell to their knees clumsily onto the frosty

Ground and, heads bowed, worshipped Almighty God, thanking him and singing praises to him for watching over all His sheep with such undemanding, loving care.

* * *

The End of a Year   *Hazel Lintott*

I love to see a grey and misty sky,
A silky thread of smoke in breathless air,
As stealthily veiled winter's icy grip
Spreads crystalline across the barren land.

On days like these when light is quick to fade,
And darkness wraps its silent, velvet cloak
Around the gloomy hedgerows and the trees
We see the year's completion, and its end.

As thin and watery sunlight seeps away,
We lay the year to rest on ancient ground,
And shower it with memories sad and sweet
While winter arches over like a shroud.

The old year's gone, but at that hour we see,
Another one arise, from last year grown.
This fresh new year will root through ages past
And feed on memory's rich and precious loam.

* * *

Index By Author

Just Write

Key: **P**=Poem **S**=Short Story **T**=Ten-Word Story/Poem

u3a

The u3a is a self-help organisation, based in the UK, for people who are no longer in employment. The aim is that people come together to further their social, educational and creative interests in a friendly and informal environment.

It is organised into more than 1,000 local u3a's run by their members for the members. Within each u3a, members help each other in learning groups from Architecture and Biology, through Badminton and Short Tennis; Bridge, Chess, and Canasta; Art, Photography and Writing through to Yoga and Zoology and almost any topic you'd like to think of in between.

In any week there are at least 10,000 interest groups taking place in the UK. The u3a helps its members form lasting friendships together with a sense of community and social wellbeing, fellowship and belonging.

u3a stands for 'University of the Third Age' which is the name under which it began. It is an international movement which has its roots in Toulouse, France in 1973. Different versions of u3a are to be found in many countries worldwide.

Proceeds from the sale of this book will go to Haywards Heath u3a.

* * *

Printed in Great Britain
by Amazon